CRAZY ON YOU

Also by Rachel Gibson

CRAZY ON YOU

RACHEL GIBSON

AVONIMPULSE

An Imprint of HarperCollinsPublishers

Excerpt from *Rescue Me* copyright © 2012 by Rachel Gibson

EPub Edition MAY 2012 ISBN: 9780062130860

Print Edition ISBN: 9780062130877

10 9 8 7 6 5 4

CHAPTER ONE

Lily Darlington hated being called crazy. She'd rather someone call her a bitch—or even a stupid bitch—because she knew she was neither and never had been. Not on purpose anyway. But put the c-word in front of bitch, and Lily was likely to go all *crazy* bitch on someone's ass.

At least she had in the past, when she'd been more impulsive and let her feelings and emotions control her. When she'd gone from zero to ten in under five seconds. When she'd dumped milk on Jimmy Joe Jenkin's head in the third grade and let air out of Sarah Little's bike tires in the sixth. When she'd thought that every action deserved a reaction. When she'd been reckless and occasionally over the top—like when she drove her Ford Taurus into her ex-husband's front room.

But she hadn't done anything over the top recently. These days, she was able to control her feelings and emotions. These days she was a respectable businesswoman and mother of a ten-year-old son. She was thirty-eight, and she'd worked hard to get the *crazy* out of her life and off the front of her name.

Lily grabbed her tote and rushed out the back of Lily Belle's Salon Day Spa. Her last cut-and-color appointment had taken longer than expected, and it was already past seven. She had to drive sixty-five miles, make dinner for her son, help him with his homework, and force him into the tub. Once he was in bed, she had to put together all the gift bags for her spa event next Saturday night.

A single bulb glowed above her head as she locked the door. Cold night air touched her cheeks and a slight breeze caught the tails of her wool coat. It was late March in the Texas panhandle and still cold enough at night that her breath hung in front of her face.

From as far back as she could remember, people had called her crazy. Crazy Lily Brooks. Then she'd married that rat bastard Ronny Darlington and they'd called her Crazy Lily Darlington.

The sound of her boot heels as she walked to her Jeep Cherokee echoed off of the Dumpster. With her thumb on the keypad, she unlocked the doors and the back hatch popped up. She set her heavy tote next to boxes filled with skin and hair care products, then reached over her head and closed the door.

Okay, so maybe she'd been just a *little* crazy during her marriage, but her ex-husband had made her crazy. He'd skirted around with half the female population of Lovett, Texas. He'd lie and tell her she was imagining things. He'd been so good at sneaking around that she'd almost convinced herself that she *was* imagining things. Then he'd dumped her for Kelly the Skank. She didn't even remember Kelly's last name, but he'd moved out and left Lily behind without so much as a backward glance. He'd also left her with a pile of bills, a bare refrigerator, and a two-year-old boy.

He'd thought he could just move on. He'd thought he could get away with making a fool of her. He'd thought she'd just take it, and *that*, more than anything, had made her drive her car through his living room. She hadn't been trying to kill him or anyone else. He hadn't even been home at the time. She'd just wanted to let him know she wasn't disposable. That he couldn't just walk away without suffering like she was suffering. But he hadn't suffered. Lily ended up in the hospital with a concussion and broken leg, and he didn't give a shit about anything but his busted TV.

She shut herself inside her SUV and fired it up. The red Cherokee was the first new car she'd ever bought. Up until a year ago, she'd always bought used. But with the success of her salon and day spa, Lily was able to splurge on something that had always been a dream—one she'd never thought would actually come true. Twin headlights shone on the back of the spa as she reversed out of the parking lot and headed home—toward the small three-bedroom house right next to her mother's, in Lovett, in the little town north of Amarillo where she was born and raised.

Living next to her mother was both a curse and a blessing. A curse because Louella Brooks was retired with nothing to do but pry into everyone's business; a blessing because Luella was retired and could watch Pippen when he got out of school. And as much as her mother drove her insane, with her "yard" art and rambling stories, she was a good grandmother and it was nice not to have to worry about her son.

Lily eased onto the highway toward Lovett and switched

on the radio to a country station. She'd never wanted to raise her son alone; she was raised by a single mother herself. Louella worked hard to support Lily and her older sister, Daisy, pouring coffee and slinging chicken fried steak for long hours at the Wild Coyote Diner. She wanted better for own child—Phillip Ronald Darlington, or, as everyone called him, Pippen. Lily was twenty-eight when she gave birth to him. She'd already known her three-year marriage was in trouble but held on desperately, trying hard to keep her family together to give her son something she'd never had—a daddy and a stay-at-home mom. She'd overlooked a lot for that to happen, only to watch Ronnie walk out on her and Pip in the end anyway.

At seven P.M., the traffic to Lovett was sparse to nonexistent, and as she drove her headlights flared on asphalt and sagebrush. She turned off the radio, fiddled around with her iPod, and sang along with Rascal Flatts. The posted speed limit was seventy, which really meant seventy-five. Everyone knew that, and she accelerated to a reasonable seventy-six.

For a year after her divorce, she might have gone a *bit . . .* wild. She might have been impulsive and emotional. Might have been lost; might have been fired from a few too many jobs; tossed back a few too many tequila shots and slept with a few too many men. Might have made a few rash decisions— like the Lily tattoo next to her hipbone and her breast augmentation. But it wasn't like she'd gone stripper-huge. She'd gone from a B-cup after the birth of her son to the full C she'd been before. Now she hated having spent money on a tattoo, and was also ambivalent about the money used on her boobs. If at a better place in her life, she might not have done it. If she'd had the confidence she had now, she might have spent the money on something more practical. Then again, Lily liked how she looked and didn't really regret it. At the time, Crazy Lily Darlington's new boobs had been the talk of the small town. Or, at least, of the Road Kill Bar where she'd spent too much time looking for Mr. Right, only to hook up with yet another Mr. Wrong.

Lily didn't really like to look back at that year of her life. She hadn't been the best mother, but supposed it was something she had to work out to get where she was today. Something she had to live through before she got her head straight and could think of her and Pip's future. Something to get out of her system before she went to cosmetology school, got her license, and built up a clientele.

Now seven years after she'd rolled her first perm and butchered her first head of hair, she was the owner of a salon—Lily Belle's, where other stylists, massage therapists, manicurists, and aestheticians rented chairs and rooms from her. She was finally doing good. So good she no longer used her caller ID to screen bill collectors.

She thought about everything she had yet to do that night and hoped her mother had fed Pippen dinner by now. The kid was bigger than most boys his age. He was going to be as big as his daddy, the rat bastard. Although lately, Ronnie had been paying a bit more attention to his son. He was taking him next weekend, which was nice since Louella had one of her bingo nights and Lily had her spa event.

The phone in her purse and the UConnect in the vehicle rang and she glanced at the steering wheel. The Jeep was still so new to her that she often hit the wrong buttons and ended the call instead of answering. Especially at night. She hit what she hoped was the right button. "Hello?"

"When are you going to be home?" her son asked.

"I'm on my way now."

"What's for dinner?"

She smiled and reached into her purse on the seat beside her. "Grandma didn't feed you?"

Pippen sighed. "She made spaghetti."

"Oh." Louella made notoriously bad Italian. Tex-Mex too. In fact, for a woman who'd spent her life serving food, she was a bad cook.

"I'm hiding in the bathroom."

Lily laughed and pulled out a bottle of water. "I'll make you a toasted cheese and soup," she said and unscrewed the cap. Her throat was sore and she wondered if she was coming down with something. Just one of the many hazards of working around a lot of people.

"Again?"

Now it was Lily's turn to sigh. "What do you want?" She looked over the top of the bottle as she took a long drink. She didn't have time to get sick.

"Pizza."

She smiled and lowered the bottle. "Again?"

A flash of light in her rearview mirror caught her attention. A cop car followed close behind, and she slowed and waited for him to go around her. When he didn't, she shockingly realized he was after *her*. "Cryin' all night," she muttered. "He can't be serious."

"What?"

"Nothing. I have to go, Pippy." She didn't want to alarm him as she slowed. "I'll be home soon," she said and ended the call. She pulled over to the shoulder of the road, and the headlights and red and blue flashers filled the Jeep as the sheriff's vehicle stopped behind her.

There might have been a time in her life when she would have freaked out. When her heart would have raced, her pulse pounded, and her mind spun, frantically wondering what she'd been caught doing now or what might be stashed in her glove compartment or console or trunk. Those days were over, and tonight all she felt was annoyed. Which she supposed meant she was a law-abiding citizen. A grown-up at thirty-eight. Even so, she was annoyed.

She shoved the Jeep into park and hit the window button in the armrest. The window slid down and she looked in the side mirror as the sheriff's door swung open. She knew most of the Potter County deputies, had gone to school with half of them or their kin. If it was Neal Flegel or Marty Dingus pulling her over, she was going to be *very* annoyed. Neal was a friend who wouldn't think twice about pulling her over just to shoot the shit, and Marty was recently divorced. She'd cut his hair for him last week, and he'd actually groaned when she'd had him in the shampoo bowl. She didn't have time for a traffic stop so Marty could ask her out again.

A wrinkle furrowed her brow as she watched the deputy, lit from behind, move toward her. He was shorter than Marty; thinner than Neal. She could see he was wearing a brown nylon jacket and a star on his chest. He had some gadgets hooked to the collar of his coat, and his belt seemed weighted down with various cop stuff. The stream of his breath hung in the headlights behind him as he approached, the steady thump-thump-thump of his cop boots closing the distance.

"I don't believe I was speeding, Officer," she said as he stopped by her door.

"Actually, you were." The red and blue lights bounced off the side of his face. She couldn't see his features clearly, but could tell he was young. "Do you have a weapon in the vehicle, Ms. Darlington?"

Ahhh. He'd already run her license plate and knew she had a permit to carry concealed. "It's beneath my seat."

He pulled out his Maglite and shone it in her lap and between her feet.

"You won't see it."

"Make sure I don't." He angled the light on her shoulder. "I need to see your driver's license, registration, and proof of insurance."

She grabbed her purse and pulled out her wallet. "You talk too fast to be from around here." She slipped out her driver license and her insurance card. "You must be new in town."

"I've been in Potter County a few weeks."

"That explains it." She reached for her registration in the glove compartment, then handed everything over. "No one gets pulled over for going five miles over the limit."

"That isn't why I pulled you over." He shined his light on her information. "You crossed the center lane several times."

Seriously? So, she wasn't the best driver when she tried to do two things at once. That's why she got the UConnect hands-free system. "There's no one else on the road for ten miles," she pointed out. "I wasn't in any danger of a head-on."

"That doesn't make it okay to take your half out of the middle."

She looked up and into the dark shadows of his face—and to where the light touched his clean-shaven chin, square jaw, and a mouth made impressive by the shadow across the bow of his upper lip. The rest of him was hidden within the inky night, but she got the distinct impression that he was not only young, but very hot. The kind of hot that in her younger days might have made her fluff her hair. These days she felt nothing but a longing for home and her old flannel pj's. She should probably feel sad about that but didn't.

"Have you had anything to drink tonight?"

She smiled. "Just water." She remembered the last time Neal had given her a ride home from the Road Kill Bar.

"Is something funny?"

And the many times she'd run home from parties, diving into bed as her mom got up for work in the morning. "Yeah," she said and started to chuckle.

Only he didn't laugh. "I'll be right back," he said and headed to his cruiser with her info.

She leaned her head back and rolled the window up. The deputy was wasting her time, and she thought of her son and dinner. All he ever seemed to want these days was pizza, but that was Pip. He got something into his head, and had hard time getting it back out.

So far Pippen was a good kid. True, he was only ten, but with her and Ronnie Darlington for parents, hell-raising had to be in his DNA. The only time she saw any sort of aggression was when Pip played sports. He loved sports, all kinds—even bowling. And he was very competitive, which normally wouldn't be a bad thing, but Pip was *hyper*competitive. He thought that if he was really good at sports, his daddy would come to his games. There were two problems with his scheme. Pip hadn't grown into himself, could hardly walk without tripping. He was awkward and, so far, a serial bench warmer. But even if he had been the best at everything, Ronny was too selfish to think about his son's football or basketball games.

A knock on the window drew her attention to the left and she hit the power button. "Find any outstanding warrants?" she asked, knowing the answer.

"Not today." He handed her information back through the window. "I pulled you over for inattentive driving, but I'm not going to ticket you."

She supposed she should say something. "Thanks"—she guessed—"Officer . . . ?"

"Matthews. Stay on your side of the road, Lily. You want to be around to raise that son." He turned on his heels and walked back to his cruiser, the crunch of gravel beneath his heels.

He knew she had a son? She put the Jeep into drive and eased back onto the highway. How? Was that sort of info available when he pulled up her driver's license number? Had he checked her weight? She glanced in her rearview mirror. He was still parked on the side of the road but had turned off his flashing lights. Like most women, she listed her weight five pounds less. She didn't actually weigh 125, but wanted to. It seemed to her that once she hit thirty-five, she gained an extra five pounds that she just couldn't lose. Of course, having a ten-year-old boy who needed snacks in the house didn't help.

Within a few moments Lily had forgotten about Officer

Matthews. She had other things to worry about, and ten minutes later, she hit the opener clipped to her visor, drove past the basketball hoop planted next to the driveway, and continued into her garage. She was sure Pippen was next door, peering out the front window, and would be home before she set down her tote and purse.

As predicted—"Mom," he called out as he burst through the back door. "Grandma said she's coming over with her extra spaghetti." He tossed his backpack onto the kitchen table. "Hide."

Crap. She reached into her purse and pulled out her cell phone. "Hi, Ma," she said as soon as her mother picked up. "Pippen said you were bringing over spaghetti. I wish I'd known because I got some takeout from Chicken Lickin'."

"Oh, darn it. I know how much you love my spaghetti." Lily didn't know where she got that idea. "Did I tell you about your new neighbor?"

Lily rolled her eyes and unbuttoned her coat. The house on her left had been for sale for over a year. It had just sold a few weeks ago, and she wondered what had taken Louella so long to introduce herself and get the lowdown.

"It's a single fella with a cat named Pinky."

A man with a cat? Named Pinky? "Is he gay?"

"Didn't appear to be, but you remember Milton Farley."

"No." She didn't care either, but there was no stopping Louella when she had a story to tell.

"He lived over on Ponderosa and was married to Brenda Jean. They had those skinny little kids with runny noses. A few—"

Lily put her hand over the mouthpiece of the phone and

whispered to her son, who'd wrapped his arms around her waist, "I'm going to hell for lying to your grandma for you."

Pippen lifted his face from the front of her shirt. He grinned and showed a mouthful of braces with blue bands. Sometimes he looked so much like his daddy it broke her heart. Golden hair, brown eyes, and long sweeping lashes. "I love you, Mama," he said, warming her heart. She would gladly go to hell for Pip. Walk through fire, kill, steal, and lie to her mother for her son. He was going to grow up strong and healthy and go to Texas A&M.

Phillip "Pippen" Darlington was going to be somebody. Somebody better than his parents.

While her mother prattled on about Milton Farley and his hidden boyfriends in Odessa, Lily bent and kissed the top of her son's head. She scratched his back through his Texas A&M sweatshirt and felt him shiver. Ronnie Darlington was a rat bastard for sure, but he'd given her a wonderful little boy. She hadn't always been the best mother, but she thanked God she'd never messed up so bad that she'd messed up her son's life.

". . . and you just know he was tricking everyone with his . . ."

Lily closed her eyes and breathed in the scent of Pippen's hair. She'd made sure that her son didn't go to school and have to hear stories about his weird mama. She knew what that was like. And she'd worked hard to make damn sure she never embarrassed him, and that he never had to hear other kids calling his mama Crazy Lily Darlington.

CHAPTER TWO

Fingers of gray crept across Lovett, Texas, as Officer Tucker Matthews pulled his Toyota Tundra into the garage and cut the engine. Full dawn was still half an hour to the east and the temperature hovered just above freezing.

He grabbed his small duffle and the service Glock from the seat next to him. He'd just started his third week with the Potter County Sheriff's Office and was pulling his second twelve-hour night shift. He moved into the kitchen and set the duffle and pistol on the counter. Pinky meowed from the vicinity of the cat condo in the living room, then ran into the kitchen to greet him.

"Hang on, Pinkster," he said and shrugged out of his brown service coat. He hung it on a hook beside the back door, then moved to the refrigerator. The veterinarian had told him milk wasn't good for Pinky, but she loved it. He poured some two-percent into a little dish on the floor as the pure black cat with the pink nose rubbed against his leg. She purred and he scratched the top of her head. A little over a year ago, he hadn't even liked cats. He'd been living on base at Fort Bliss, ready to be discharged from the Army after ten years of service and preparing to move in with his girlfriend, Tiffany, and her cat, Pinky. Two weeks after he moved in with her, she moved out—taking his Gibson custom Les Paul guitar and leaving behind her cat.

Tucker rose and moved back across the kitchen. At that point, he'd had two choices: reenlist or do something else with his life. He loved the Army. The guys were his brothers. The commanding officers, the only real father figures he'd ever known. He'd enlisted at the age of eighteen, and the Army had been his only family. But it was time to move on. To do something besides blow shit up and take bullets. And there was nothing like a bullet to the head to make a guy realize that he actually did care if he lived or died. Until he'd felt the blood run down his face, he hadn't thought he cared. It wasn't like there was anyone but his Army buddies who gave a shit anyway.

Then he met Tiffany, and thought she cared. Some of the guys had warned him that she was an Army groupie, but he didn't listen. He'd met groupies, swam a few times in the groupie pool, but with Tiffany he'd been fooled into believing she cared about him, that she wanted more than a soldier deployed months at a time. Maybe he wanted to be fooled. In the end, he guessed she'd cared more about his guitar. At first, he was pissed. What kind of person abandoned a little cat? Leaving it with *him*? A guy who'd never had any sort of pet and didn't have a clue what to do with one? Now, he figured, Tiffany had done him a favor.

So what did a former Army gunner do once he was discharged? Enroll in the El Paso County Sheriff's Academy, of course. The six-month training program had been a piece of cake for him, and he graduated at the top of his class. Once his probationary period was over, he applied for a position in Potter County, and, a few months ago, moved to Lovett.

Sunlight spread across his backyard and into the neighbors'. He'd bought his first house a few weeks ago. His home. He was thirty, and except for the first five years of his life, when he'd lived with his grandmother, this was the first home to which he truly belonged. He wasn't an outsider. A squatter. This wasn't temporary shelter until he was shuffled off to another foster home.

He was home. He felt it in his bones and he didn't know why. He'd lived in different parts of the country—of the world—but Lovett, Texas, had felt right the moment he arrived. He recognized Lily Darlington's red Jeep even before he ran her plates. For the past week, since he moved in, he'd be getting ready to hit the sack as she backed out of her driveway with her kid in the car.

Before he shined his light into her car, the impression of his neighbor was . . . single mother with big blond curls and a long, lean body. After the traffic stop, he knew she was thirty-eight, older than she looked and prettier than he'd imagined from his quick glimpses of her. And she'd clearly been annoyed that he had the audacity to pull her over. He was used to that, though. Generally people weren't happy to see the rolling lights in their rearview.

Across his yard and Lily's, separated by a short white fence, his kitchen window faced into hers. Today was Saturday. There weren't any lights on yet, but he knew that by ten that boy of hers would be outside bouncing a basketball in the driveway and keeping him awake.

He'd been out of the Army for two years but was still a very light sleeper. One small sound and he was wide awake, pinpointing the position, origin, and exact nature of the sound.

He replaced Pinky's milk, then she followed him out of the kitchen and into the living room. A remote control sat on the coffee table he'd made from a salvaged old door. He'd sanded and varnished it until it was smooth as satin.

Tucker loved working with his hands. He loved taking a piece of old wood and making it into something beautiful. He reached for the remote and turned the big screen TV to a national news channel. Pinky jumped up onto the couch beside him as he leaned over and untied his tactical boots. A deep purr rattled her chest as she squeezed her little black body between his arm and chest. With his attention on the screen across the room and the latest news out of Afghanistan, he finished with one boot and started on the other. The picture of tanks and troops in camouflage brought back memories of restlessness, violence, and boredom. Of knocking down doors, shooting anything that moved, and watching his buddies die. Adrenaline, fear closing his throat, and blood.

Pinky bumped the top of her head against his chin and he moved his head from side to side to avoid her. The things he'd seen and done in the military had certainly affected him. Had changed him, but not like some of the guys he knew. Probably because he had his share of trauma and stress before signing up. By eighteen, he'd been a pro at handling whatever life threw his way. He knew how to shut it down and let it all roll right off.

He hadn't come out of the military with PTSD like some

of the guys. Oh, sure he'd been jumpy and on edge, but after a few months, he'd adjusted to civilian life. Perhaps because his whole life had been one adjustment after another.

Not anymore, though. "Jesus, Pink." The cat's purring and bumping got so annoying he picked her up and set her on the couch beside him. Of course she didn't stay and crawled right back onto his lap. He sighed and scratched her back. Somehow he'd let an eight-pound black cat with a pink nose totally run his life. He wasn't sure how that had even happened. He used to think cats were for old ladies or ugly chicks or gay men. The fact that he had a five-foot-square cat condo that he'd built himself, and a pantry stocked with cat treats, pretty much shot his old prejudice all to hell. He wasn't an old lady or ugly or gay. He did draw the line at cat outfits, though.

He stripped down to his work pants and the cold-weather base layer he wore beneath his work shirt. He made himself a large breakfast of bacon and eggs and juice. As he rinsed the dishes, he heard the first thud of the neighbor's basketball. It was eight thirty. The kid was at it earlier than usual. Tucker glanced out the window that faced the neighbor's driveway. The kid's blond hair stuck up in the back. He wore a silver Dallas Cowboys parka and a pair of red sweatpants.

When Tucker worked the night shift, he liked to be in bed before ten and up by four. He could wear earplugs, but he'd rather not. He didn't like the idea of one of his senses being dulled while he slept. He pulled on his jogging shoes and a gray hooded sweatshirt. If he talked to the kid, maybe they could work something out.

He hit the garage door opener on his way out and moved into the driveway. The cold morning chilled his hands, and his breath hung in front of his face. He moved toward the boy, across a strip of frozen grass, as the steady bounce-bounce-bounce of the ball and the sound of it hitting the backboard filled his ears.

"Hey, buddy," he said as he stopped in his neighbor's drive. "It's kind of cold to be playing so early."

"I got to be the best," he said, his breath streaming behind him as he tried for a layup and missed. The ball hit the rim and the kid caught it before it hit the ground. "I'm going to be the best at school."

Tucker stuck his hands in the pockets of his sweatshirt. "You're going to freeze your nuts off, kid."

The boy stopped and looked up at him. His clear brown eyes widened as he stuck the ball under one arm of his puffy coat. "Really?"

No. Not really. Tucker shrugged. "I wouldn't risk it. I'd wait until around three or four when it warms up."

The kid tried a jump shot that slid around the rim. "Can't. It's the weekend. I gotta practice as much as I can."

Crap. Tucker bent down and grabbed the ball as it rolled by his foot. He supposed he could threaten to give the kid some sort of citation or scare him with the threat of arrest. But Tucker didn't believe in empty threats or abusing his power over the powerless. He knew what that felt like. And telling the kid he was going to freeze his nuts off, didn't count. That could really happen here in the Texas panhandle. Especially when the wind started blowing. "What's your name?"

"Phillip Darlington, but everyone calls me Pippen."

Tucker stuck out his free hand. "Tucker Matthews. How old are you Pippen?"

"Ten."

Tucker was no expert, but the kid seemed tall for his age.

"My grandma says you named your cat Pinky. That's a weird name."

This from a kid named Pippen? Tucker bounced the ball a few times. "Whose your grandma?"

"Louella Brooks. She lives on the other side of me and my mom." He pointed behind him with his thumb.

Ah. The older lady who talked nonstop and had given him a pecan pie. "We have a problem."

"We do?" He sniffed and wiped the back of his hand across his red nose.

"Yeah. I've got to sleep and you bouncing this ball is keeping me awake."

"Put a pillow over your head." He tilted his chin to one side. "Or you could turn on the TV. My mom has to sleep with the TV on sometimes."

Neither was an option. "I've got a better idea. We play a game of H-O-R-S-E. If I win, you wait until three to play. If you win, I'll put a pillow over my head."

Phillip shook his head. "You're a grown-up. That's not fair."

Damn. "I'll spot you the first three letters."

The kid looked at his fingers and counted. "I only have to make two baskets?"

"Yep." Tucker wasn't worried. He'd been watching the kid for a couple of days and he sucked. He tossed the kid the ball. "I'll even let you go first."

"Okay." Pippen caught the ball and moved to an invisible free-throw line. His breath hung in front of his face, his eyes narrowed, and he bounced the ball in front of him. He got into an awkward free-throw stance, shot, and totally wafted it. The ball missed the backboard and Tucker tried not to smile as he ran into his own driveway to retrieve it. He dribbled back and did a left-handed layup. "That's an H," he said and tossed the ball to Pippen. The boy tried his luck at a layup and missed.

Tucker hit a jump shot at the center key. "O."

"Wow." Pippen shook his head. "You're good."

He'd played a lot of b-ball on his downtime in the military, and it didn't hurt that the kid's hoop was lowered to about eight feet and there was no one playing defense.

The kid moved to the spot where Tucker had stood. Once again his eyes narrowed and he bounced the ball in front of him. He lined up the shot and Tucker sighed.

"Keep your elbows pointed straight," he heard himself coach. God, he couldn't believe he was giving the kid pointers. He wasn't even sure he liked kids. He'd never really been around any since he'd been one himself, and most of those had been like him. Throwaways.

Pippen held the ball right in front of his face and pointed his elbows at the net.

"No." Tucker moved behind the kid, lowered the ball a few inches, and moved his cold hands to the correct position. "Keep the ball lined up, bend your knees, and shoot."

"Pippen!"

Both Tucker and the boy spun around at the same time. Lily Darlington stood behind them, wrapped up in a red wool coat and wearing white bunny slippers. Crisp morning light caught in her blond hair curled up in big Texas-size rollers.

The chilled air caught in his lungs and turned her cheeks pink. She was pretty, even if her ice blue gaze cut Tucker to shreds. She stared at him as she spoke to her child. "I called your name twice."

"Sorry." The kid dribbled the ball. "I was practicing my shots."

"Go eat your breakfast. Your waffles are getting cold."

"I have to practice."

"Basketball season is over until next year."

"That's why I have to practice. To get better."

"You have to go eat. Right now."

Pippen gave a long suffering sigh and tossed the ball to Tucker. "You can play if you want."

He didn't, but he caught the ball. "Thanks. See ya around, Pippen."

As the kid stormed past his mother, she reached out and grabbed him. She hugged him close and kissed the top of his head. "You don't have to be the best at everything, Pip." She pulled back and looked into his eyes. "I love you bigger than the sun and stars."

"I know."

"Forever and ever. Always." She moved her palms to his cheek. "You're a good boy"—she smiled into his upturned face—"with dirty hands. Wash them when you go inside."

Tucker looked at her slim hands on the boy's cheeks and temples, cupping his ears. Her nails were red and her skin looked soft. A thin blue vein lined her wrist and disappeared beneath the cuff of her red wool coat. The chilly air in his lungs burned. "Go inside or you'll freeze your ears off."

"My nuts."

Uh-oh.

"What?"

"I'll freeze my nuts off." He glanced behind his shoulder and laughed. "Tucker said it's so cold out here I'll freeze my nuts off."

Her gaze cut to his and one brow rose up her forehead. "Charming." She ran her fingers through her son's short hair. "Go eat before your waffles are as cold as your . . . ears." The kid took off and she folded her arms across her chest. The curlers in her hair should have made her look ridiculous. They didn't. They made him want to watch her take them out. It was silly, and he dribbled he ball instead of thinking about her hair. "You must be the new neighbor."

"Tucker Matthews." He stuck the ball under one arm and offered his free hand. She looked at it for several heartbeats then shook it. Her skin was as warm and soft as it looked; he wondered what her palm would feel like on the side of his face. Then he wondered why he was wondering about her at all.

"Lily Darlington." Her blue eyes stared into his, and she obviously didn't recognize him from the night before. She took her hand back and slid it into her pocket. "I'm sure you're perfectly nice, but I'm very protective and I don't let just any man around my son."

That was wise, he supposed. "Are you worried about me doing something to your kid?"

She shook her head. "Not worried. Just letting you know that I protect Pip."

Then maybe she shouldn't have named him Pip because that was just a guaranteed ass-kicking. Then again, this was

Texas. The rule for names in Texas was different from the rest of the country. A guy named Guppy couldn't exactly beat the crap out of a Pip. "I'm not going to hurt your kid." He folded his arms and rocked back on his heels.

"Just so we're clear, if you even think about hurting one hair on his head, I'll kill you and not lose a wink of sleep over it."

For some perverse reason, the threat made him like her. "You don't even know me."

"I know that you're playing basketball with a ten-year-old at nine o'clock in the morning," she said, her accent thick with warning. "It's about thirty-two degrees, and you're talking about your freezing nuts with my son. That's not exactly normal behavior for an adult man."

Since she obviously lived alone, he had to wonder if she knew anything about normal behavior for an adult man. "I'm playing basketball and freezing my nuts off so I can get some sleep. I just got off work and your kid's basketball keeps me awake. I thought if I played a game of H-O-R-S-E, he'd cut me a break." That was close enough to the truth.

She blinked. "Oh." She tilted her head to one side and a wrinkle pulled her brows as if she were suddenly trying to place him in her memory. "You work the night shift at the meat packing plant? I worked there for a few weeks about five years ago."

"No." He dribbled the ball a few times and waited.

"Hmm." Her brow smoothed and she turned to go. "I've got to see to Pip. It was nice to meet you, Mr. Matthews."

"We met last night."

She turned back and once again her brows were drawn.

"I pulled you over for inattentive driving."

Her lips parted. "That was you?"

"Yeah." He shook his head. "You're a shitty driver, Lily."

"You're a sheriff?"

"Deputy."

"That explains the tragic pants."

He looked down at his dark brown trousers with the beige stipe up the outside legs. "You don't think they're hot."

She shook her head. "Sorry."

He tossed her the ball and she caught it. "Tell Pippen that if he cuts me a break tomorrow morning, I'll teach him how to slam dunk tomorrow afternoon around four."

"I'll tell him."

"You're not afraid I'm a pervert?"

"Pippen knows he can't leave the yard without telling me or his grandma." She shrugged. "And you already know I'm licensed to carry concealed. I've got a Beretta 9mm subcompact." She stuck the ball under one arm. "Just so you know."

"Nice." He managed not to laugh. "But are you bragging or threatening a law officer?"

"Pippen's daddy isn't really in the picture. I'm all he's got and it's my job to make sure he's safe and happy."

"He's lucky to have you."

"I'm lucky to have him."

Tucker watched her go, then turned and walked back to his house. Only one person in his entire life had made sure he was safe. His grandmother Betty. If he thought hard, he could recall the touch of her soft hand on his head and back. But Betty had died three days after Tucker turned five.

He moved into his kitchen and pulled his sweatshirt over his head. His mother had split when he was a baby and he had no memory of her. Just photographs. He didn't know who his father was and doubted his mother had *ever* known. She'd finally killed herself with a drug cocktail when Tucker was three. As a kid, he'd wondered about her; wondered what his life would have been like if she hadn't been an addict. As an adult, he just felt disgust—disgust for a woman who cared more about drugs than her son.

He turned off the television on his way to his bedroom and kicked off his shoes. After Betty's death, he'd been shipped off to aunts who didn't want or care about him; and by the time he turned ten, he was turned over to the state of Michigan and shuffled through the foster care system.

He took off his pants and tossed them into the hamper he used for dry cleaning. No one had wanted to adopt a ten-year-old with his history and bad attitude. He'd spent most of the years between the ages of ten and sixteen in and out of foster homes and juvenile court, which finally landed him in a halfway house run by a retired Vietnam vet. Elias Peirce had been a no-bullshit hard-ass with strict rules. But he'd been fair. The first time Tucker had given him lip, he gave Tucker an old cane-back chair and a pack of sandpaper. "Make it as smooth as a baby's backside," he'd barked. It had taken him a week, but after his daily homework and chores were done, Tucker sanded until the chair felt like silk beneath his hands. Following the chair, he'd made a bookcase and a small table.

Tucker couldn't say that he and Elias Peirce had been as close as father and son, but he changed Tucker's life and never treated him like a throwaway kid. Elias made him work out the pent-up anger and aggression just below his skin in a constructive way.

Tucker didn't like to talk about his past—didn't really talk about his life. During the course of normal conversation, whenever anyone asked about his life, he just said he didn't have much family and changed the subject.

He thought of Lily Darlington and the way she touched Pippen. The way she looked into his eyes and touched his cheek and told him she loved him bigger than the stars. Tucker was sure his grandmother had loved him, but he was equally sure she'd never threatened to kick ass on his behalf. He'd had to kick ass on his own behalf. He'd always had to take care of himself.

He was a man now—thirty years old—and he was the man he was because of the life he'd been dealt. He knew a lot of guys who'd come back from Iraq or Afghanistan and had a hard time adjusting to life outside of the military. Not Tucker. At least not as much. He'd learned long ago how to deal with shit thrown at him. How to cope with trauma and how to let it go. Oh, he had some really dark memories, but he didn't live with them. He'd worked them out and moved on.

He stripped to his gray boxers and climbed into bed. Everything he had, he'd earned. No one had given him anything and he was a content man. He fell asleep within minutes of his head hitting the pillow, and at some point, when he was warm and comfy and deep into REM, Lily Darlington entered his dreams. She wore red silk and her hands touched his face and neck. She looked into his eyes and smiled as she cupped his cheek. "You're cold, Tucker," she said. "You need to warm up." The dream started nice and innocent but quickly turned hot and dirty. Her hands slid across his chest as she lowered her

CHAPTER THREE

True to his word, that Sunday afternoon at around four P.M., Deputy Tucker Matthews knocked on Lily's front door. She opened it and stood in stunned silence, like she'd suffered a blow to the head.

"Is Pippen around?" He had a new basketball tucked under one arm and a pair of silver aviators covered his eyes— eyes that were a warm brown and creased at the corners when he was amused, like when she'd threated to shoot him the other morning.

Lily was so shocked stupid that he'd kept his word that all she could utter was "Ahhh, yeah." Her shock couldn't have anything to do with him looking so good. She'd seen him yesterday, knew he was good-looking. A scar creased his forehead from the middle of his right brow to the line of his short brown hair. This, along with his rough, masculine edges, kept him from being a pretty boy, but allowed him enough intrigue to give a girl bad thoughts about body searches. So why did she feel so rattled today? He was wearing that same hideous gray Army sweatshirt he'd had on yesterday, with frayed mouth to the side of his neck, and the things she whispered against his throat weren't in the least innocent.

"I want you," she whispered as her palm moved over his chest, down the side of his waist, then back up again. "Do you want me?" Her touch was soft and slow, frustrating, sliding back and forth and driving him mad.

"Yes. God, yes." He ran his fingers through her hair, bunching it in his hands as she kissed his neck and inched her hot palm lower—lower, down his stomach and belly until her fingernails scraped his skin just above the elastic of his underwear.

Her fingers slide beneath the elastic waistband and she wrapped her soft warm hand around his extremely tight erection. "You're a good boy with dirty hands."

His heart pounded in his chest as he shoved her against the wall and into her. All caveman aggression and hunger. In his dream she loved every second of it. She met every hard plunge of his hard dick with insatiable greed, shoving her hips into his, begging for more and moaning his name. "Tucker!" she screamed in his head—and his eyes flew open. He sat up in bed, his lungs pulling oxygen into his chest and his pulse pounding in his ears.

A sliver of light sneaked beneath his blackout blinds and streaked across the dark room. The sound of his heavy breathing filled the space around him. He'd just had a wild sex dream about Lily Darlington. Obviously he'd gone without for too long, and he'd lost his mind. He didn't know her. She was a single mother. He felt like a pervert.

A pervert who needed to get laid before he lost his mind again.

sleeves, a torn neck—and he looked like he'd just dragged himself out of bed. He was all rough and scruffy and definitely needed to shave. "You're here," she managed.

"I told you I would be."

Lily was five feet six inches tall and she noticed he was just a few inches taller—perhaps five ten. What he lacked in height, he made up for in pure, unadulterated hotness. So much hotness that it lit a little fire in her stomach and heated up her pulse. She held the door open for him and shocked herself further by wondering what he'd look like with that horribly ratty sweatshirt ripped off and his wrist cuffed to something. "Come in and I'll get him."

He took a step back instead. She couldn't see his eyes but color crept up his neck to his cheeks as if he'd read her mind. "Tell him I'll be in the driveway warming up," he said and turned to go.

No doubt, her inappropriate thoughts were written on her face and scared him. They scared her too. "Pippen," she called out over her shoulder, "Deputy Matthews is here for you."

He stopped a few steps down and glanced back at her. "You can call me Tucker."

No. No, she couldn't. The guy was probably all of twenty-five, and she was thinking of him shirtless and cuffed to a bedpost. It made her feel a bit pervy. Although, to be fair to herself, she'd never had such a good-looking guy show up on her porch before. Not even when she'd been twenty-five. Not even the rat bastard she'd married, Ronnie. And even though she hated to admit it now, Ronnie had been damn fine.

"I'm coming," Pippen hollered as he raced past his mother, shoving his arms into his jacket.

Lily shut the door behind her and leaned against it. Well, that had been weird and awkward. Yesterday she'd been fine. She'd seen him, seen that he looked much more like a faux cop from a *Playgirl* magazine than a real one. She'd acknowledged his good looks to herself, thought about body searches, *and* managed to speak like an intelligent woman. At least today she didn't have rollers in her hair and half her makeup on her face.

Her hair was pulled back in a ponytail, and she was wearing a white cable knit sweater, jeans, and a brown woven belt around her hips. If she'd known company would appear on her porch, she would have done her hair and put on some lipstick.

She pushed away from the door and moved across the living room to the couch. On the top of the oak coffee table and across the back of the red sofa sat little teal bags with the logo of Lily's spa embossed in white in each center. Several rolls of teal-and-white cellophane and bags of trail-size beauty products lay on the couch cushions. She moved the rolls aside and sat.

Tucker Matthews wasn't company. He was the next door neighbor who was playing basketball with Pippen in the afternoon so he could sleep in the morning. He'd given Pip his word and he'd kept it, which was more than she could say for her son's father, who didn't pay attention to trivial things like court orders and visitation and keeping his word. He worked on Ronnie-time, which usually depended on the latest slootie pants he'd hooked up with.

Yesterday, when Lily had walked outside and seen a stranger in her driveway playing ball with her son, she'd been a bit freaked out. Today she wasn't sure how she felt about it. Pip wanted a father so desperately. He loved any male attention, and would be crushed when the deputy tired of playing, took his ball and went home for good.

Lily rose from the couch and moved into her shiny white kitchen with yellow cupboards. She'd deal with that when it happened. God knew Pippen needed some testosterone around him, if only for a few hours. He spent most of his time with her and his grandmother. Occasionally, he spent time with her sister Daisy's husband, Jack, and their son, Nathan, when he was home from college. Daisy and Jack had a six-year-old daughter and another one on the way.

Lily went to the kitchen sink and leaned across as far as she could. She pushed aside a bamboo plant, a pinch pot, and one side of her daisy-print curtains. She could see just a sliver of the driveway with the basketball hoop. The ball hit the backboard and bounced off.

She could clearly hear the steady bounce of the ball and then a shot that was nothing but net. Clearly, the shot was not made by her son, who hadn't grown into himself yet.

Her cell phone on the counter rang and she glanced down at it. Ronnie. Great. He was probably calling to say he couldn't take Pippen next weekend.

"You better not be calling just to piss me off," she answered.

"Ha-ha-ha," he chuckled in that stupid Ronnie way that she used to think was so cool but now was like nails on a chalkboard. "I need to talk to Pip."

"Not if you're going to back out on next weekend, you don't."

"I'm not backin' out. I thought he might want to go see my parents in Odessa, is all."

Pip hadn't seen his grandparents in at least a year. "Seriously?"

"Yeah."

Ronnie was a deadbeat. No doubt. But Pippen thought the sun rose and sat on that rat bastard's ass. She could stand on her head and juggle cupcakes to make Pippen happy, and all his daddy had to do was pull up in his latest monster truck and Pip was in heaven.

"I'm sure he'll like that," she said as she moved out the garage door and hit a switch on the wall. "You better not back out."

"I ain't gonna back out."

"That's what you said the last time you backed out." The door slid up and she ducked beneath it and walked out onto the driveway. Her son and the deputy stood near an imaginary free throw line. "If you do, it'll be the last time, Ronnie."

"He's my son."

"Yeah. You might try and remember that on a somewhat consistent basis." The cool air touched her face and neck, and the heels of her boots tap-tapped across the concrete. "Pip. Your daddy's on the phone." She handed her son the cell and watched his little face light up.

"Tucker's winning," Pippen said, excited as a monkey on a peanut farm as he took the phone from her. "One more basket and I'm toast."

She looked toward the man standing in the middle of the driveway slowly dribbling the ball. Sunlight reflected off the lenses of his glasses and shined in his rich brown hair. "I got your back," she told her son and moved to stand in front of the deputy.

"What are you doing?"

"Making sure you don't score while Pip's on the phone." She raised her arms over her head for added measure.

"We're playing H-O-R-S-E."

She had a vague memory of H-O-R-S-E from grammar school. It had something to do with the first player to spell horse winning. She'd never played. As a Texan and a girl, she'd played volleyball. She'd been one hell of a spiker.

"There's no man-to-man in horse."

She dropped her arms. "What?"

He said it again, only this time really slow. "There's . . . no . . . man . . . to . . . man . . . in . . . H-O-R-S-E."

She still wasn't quite sure what that meant. "Are you being condescending?"

He bounced the ball and moved a few inches closer. Close enough that she had to tip her head back to look up. Close enough that she could smell sweat and clean Texas air. "No. You told me I talk fast."

"I did?" She swallowed and felt a sudden urge to take a step back. Back to a safer distance. "When?"

"The other night when I pulled you over."

She didn't remember saying that, but it was true. "Where are you from, Deputy?"

"Originally Detroit."

"Long way from home."

"For the past eleven years, I've lived at Fort Bliss, then El Paso and Houston."

"Army?"

"Staff Sergeant, Second Battalion, Third Field Artillery."

He was in the Army and now the police force? "How long were you in the military?"

"Ten years." He slowly bounced the ball. "If you want to play man-on-man, we can."

Ten years? He had to be older than he looked.

"Or man-on-woman." One dark brow rose up his forehead and his voice got kind of low and husky. "You wanna play a little man-on-woman, Lily?"

She blinked. She wasn't sure what he meant. Was he joking or was that a real position or play or whatever in basketball? "Do I have to sweat?" She didn't like to sweat in her good clothes.

"It's not good if at least one person doesn't work up a sweat."

Okay, she was pretty sure he wasn't talking about basketball. She glanced over at Pippen standing at the edge of the driveway listening to his daddy. She looked back at Tucker, at her reflection in his glasses. If she leaned forward just a bit, she could put her face in the crook of his neck just above the torn collar of his sweatshirt. Where his skin would be cool and smell like a warm man.

"You're blushing."

In his glasses, she could see the pink creeping to her cheeks. Could feel it heating her chest. He was young and attractive, and she wasn't used to men flirting with her. At least men she hadn't known most of her life. "Are you hitting on me?"

"If you have to ask, then I'm not as smooth as I think I am."

He *was* hitting on her! "But I'm a lot older than you," she blurted.

"Eight years isn't a lot."

Eight years. He knew her age. No doubt from her driver's license. She was so flustered, she could hardly do simple math. He was thirty. That was still young, but not as young as she'd thought. Not so young that thinking about him as a faux cop in *Playgirl* was perverted. Well, not all that perverted. It wasn't illegal anyway.

"Your cheeks are getting really red."

"It's chilly out here." She turned toward the house but his hand on her arm stopped her. She looked down at his long fingers on the forearm of her white sweater. She ran her gaze up the frayed wrist of his sleeve, up his arm and shoulder to the scruffy growth on his square jaw. He had the kind of mouth that would feel good sliding across her skin.

"What are you thinking, Lily?"

She looked up into this mirrored glasses. "Pure thoughts."

A deep chuckle spilled from his lips. "That makes one of us."

For the second time in less than an hour, Deputy Tucker Matthews stunned her into silence.

"Momma!" Pippen called out as he headed toward her. "Daddy and me are going to Odessa next weekend to see Memaw and Papaw."

She tore her gaze from Tucker's face. "I know, sugar." She took her cell phone from her son. "We'll pack lots of road snacks."

Pippen turned to the deputy. "Is it my shot?"

He shook his head. "Sorry. I gotta go take a shower before

work." A slight smile curved his lips. "I worked up a sweat."

"Not me," Pippen told him. "I don't sweat. I'm too little. Momma doesn't sweat either."

He raised his brows above the gold frame of his sunglasses. "That's a shame. She should do something about that."

Lily's own brows knitted and her mouth parted. Was he hitting on her in front of her son? And was she so out of practice she didn't know?

Tucker laughed and looked down at the young boy in front of him. "But I have tomorrow and Tuesday off. We can finish then."

"Okay."

He shifted the ball from one arm to the other. "See ya later, Lily."

No way could she call him Tucker. He might not be as young as she'd first thought, but he still was young and hot and an outrageous flirt. He was dangerous for a single mother in a small town. A big old hunk of hot flaming danger for a woman who'd finally lived down her wild reputation. "Deputy Matthews."

Tucker stretched his arms upward and moved his head from side to side. It was 0800 in Amarillo and he was just finishing up the paperwork from the night before. He'd made two DUI arrests, issued three moving violations, and had responded to a 10-91b in Lovett. The noisy animal in question had been a fat Chihuahua named Hector. The dog's elderly owner, Velma Patterson, had cried and promised to keep the ankle-biter quiet and Tucker had let her off with a verbal warning.

"It was that horrible Nelma Buttersford who called. Wasn't it?" Ms. Patterson wept into a rumpled tissue. "She hates Hector."

"I'm not sure who called," he'd answered.

Tucker rose from the desk. That's what he liked about working in Potter County. There wasn't a lot happening on a Sunday night. Not like Harris County. He liked the slower pace that gave him time to plow through his paperwork.

No, not much happened, and he was fine with that. He'd seen a lot of action in Iraq and Afghanistan, and later after joining the department in Houston. Here, there was just enough going on to keep him interested, but not so much that it kept him up at night.

At least not yet. But it would. Bad things happened sometimes and he'd signed up for the job to deal with them. For as long as he could remember, he'd been dealing with bad things. He knew how to survive when shit went south.

He moved to the locker room and opened the locker with his name printed on cloth tape. He unbuttoned his beige and brown long-sleeved work shirt and pulled at the Velcro tabs at his shoulders and the sides of his waist. The vest weighed a little under ten pounds. Nothing compared to the body armor he'd worn in the military. He set it inside the locker and buttoned his shirt over his black tactical undershirt.

"Hey, Matthews," Deputy Neal Flegel called out as he entered the locker room. "Did you hear about the 10-32 up at Lake Meredith?"

He'd heard the call over the radio. "Yeah. What kind of idiots are out on the lake that time of night?"

Flegel opened his locker and unbuttoned his shirt. "Two

idiots fishing in a leaky ten-foot aluminum boat, no life jackets, and a cooler full of Lone Star."

He knew from listening to the radio that they'd recovered one body close to shore. Another deputy, Marty Dingus, entered the locker room and he and Neal shot the shit like two old compadres. Brothers. Tucker had had a lot of compadres. Brothers in arms. Some of them he'd straight-up hated but would have died for. A sheriff's department wasn't unlike the military in that regard. They both played by big-boy rules. He was the new guy in Potter County. He'd been in this spot before, and he knew how to roll and adapt and get along for the sake of the job. He looked forward to getting to know the deputies here in his new home.

"How do you like Potter County so far?" Marty asked. "Not quite as hot as Harris County."

Tucker reached for his jacket inside his locker. Marty wasn't talking about the temperature. "That's what I like about it." He'd been in a enough "hot" places to last him a lifetime.

Neal peeled off his vest. "Did you find a place to live?"

Tucker nodded and shut his locker. "I took your advice and found a house in Lovett. On Winchester. Not far from the high school over there."

"Winchester?" Neal frowned in thought. Both deputies had been born and raised in Lovett and still lived there with their families. "Do we know anyone who lives on Winchester?" he asked Marty.

"Now?" Marty shrugged and shook his head. "When we were in school, the Larkins . . . Cutters . . . and the Brooks girls."

"That's why it sounds familiar." Neal set his vest inside his locker. "Lily Darlington lives on Winchester. She bought the house right next door to her mama."

Marty laughed. "Crazy Lily?"

Crazy Lily?

"Some of my earliest wet dreams involved Crazy Lily." Both men laughed and Tucker might have appreciated the humor if he hadn't recently had his own sex dream about Lily Darlington.

"She's my neighbor." Tucker shoved his arms into his jacket. "Why do you call her crazy?" She hadn't acted crazy around him. More like she'd driven *him* crazy in that white sweater yesterday. He'd taken one look at her tits in that sweater and all the blood in his head had drained to his pants.

"I don't think she's crazy these days," Neal said. "Not like when she used to dance on tables."

Lily danced on tables? "Professionally?"

"No. At parties in high school." Marty laughed. "Those long legs in a pair of tiny shorts and Justin's were something to see."

Jesus.

"She's not like that anymore," Neal defended her. "I think that concussion she got driving her car into Ronnie's front room back in '04 knocked some sense into her."

Jesus, Joseph, *and* Mary. "Who's Ronnie?"

"Her ex."

"And she drove her car into his front room? On purpose?"

"She always said her foot slipped on account of a migraine," Neal answered. Both men laughed and Neal continued: "She was never charged with anything, but everyone knows Crazy Lily Darlington drove her car into that house on purpose. She came real close to being 5150'd." Neal shrugged. "But she was already in the hospital for few days, so it didn't make sense."

5150? Tucker had picked up a 5150 last year in South Houston. The schizophrenic woman had locked herself in her bedroom for three days and had been eating her mattress.

"It was just a good thing Ronnie was off with his latest," Marty added.

Holy Jesus. He was having crazy sex dreams and lusting after a crazy woman. A woman who'd possibly tried to kill her ex by running her car into his house and had almost been locked up on a 5150 hold. That piece of info should be enough to shrivel his nuts, but it didn't. He thought of her and Pippen and her fierceness. He thought of her hands on his own chest, and his hands running up long legs, and he didn't know who was crazier. Him or Crazy Lily Darlington.

Chapter Four

Lily pulled the Jeep into her garage and left the door up. She'd dropped Pippen off at school and gone to Albertson's for a few groceries. She had a lot to do before Pippen got home from school.

She got out of the car and walked toward the curb. Pippen had been so excited after talking to Ronnie yesterday. The thought of going to Odessa with his daddy kept him wired all day and night, and he'd had a hard time falling asleep.

A big beige garbage can sat at the curb and she grabbed the handle to pull it into the garage. The cold plastic chilled her palm and she glanced up as Tucker's silver Tundra pulled into the drive next door. She quickly returned his wave and ducked her head as she tugged the big can into her garage. Pippen had gone on and on about Tucker too. Tucker was going to teach him to dunk and free throw, and juke. Whatever that meant.

She pushed the garbage can against the wall, moved to her Jeep, and opened the back. She'd listened to Pip until she hadn't been able to take it another minute. She'd spread her arms and said, "What am I? A stump full of spiders?"

Pip had rolled his eyes. "You're just my momma."

Yeah, just his momma, and he thought the sun rose and set on Ronnie's deadbeat ass. Lily grabbed the handles of two grocery bags and heard Tucker's boot heels just before his shadow fell across the threshold of the garage.

"I'll get those," he said.

She glanced across her shoulder at him as he stopped next to her in his brown jacket and tragic pants. Then she put her chin to her shoulder and glanced behind her. Tucker playing basketball in her driveway with Pippen was one thing—but carrying her groceries inside was another. She was a single mom in a small town that would never completely forget her wild past. None of the neighbors seemed to be home. "You can get the others," she said and hurried to the back door. "Thank you."

"No problem." He grabbed the remaining four bags and shut the back of the Jeep.

"Pip says you're going to teach him to dunk." She pushed a big button by the back step and the garage door slid closed.

"I'll try." He followed her into the kitchen and set the bags on the counter next to her. "He needs to work on his dribbling first."

Lily unbuttoned her navy pea coat and hung it on a hook by the door. That morning she'd dressed in her pink yoga pants, white sports bra, and Spandex tank. Later, she planned to drag out her mat, pop in her Rodney Yee DVD, and do a little downward facing dog in her living room. She looked back at Tucker's profile. At his chin and mouth and wide shoulders. Besides her brother-in-law and nephew, Pippen was the only male who'd ever been in her house. It felt weird to have Tucker there. "Thanks again."

"Thank me with coffee." He turned to face her and reached for the zipper of his dark brown jacket. His long fingers pulled the tab downward. One slow inch at a time as his eyes took a languid journey down her body, blatantly checking her out.

She should say something clever and witty or indignant, but as always with him, she couldn't think. Clearly his testosterone was throwing off the balance in the house. Throwing her off the balance. "Won't the caffeine keep you up?"

He raised his gaze to her face, pausing for a heartbeat on her lips before he looked into her eyes. "I have today and tomorrow off."

Lord love a duck, his energy caused friction in her stomach. Fiery dangerous friction that she hadn't let herself feel for a long time. She moved to the coffee maker and filled the filter with Italian roast. With Tucker, it wasn't a matter of *letting*. It was more like a bombardment. "I'm off today too. And I have a million things to do before Saturday's spa event." It wasn't necessarily a hint for him to leave. Not yet. In a few more minutes, she'd kick him out. There'd been a time in her life when she liked playing with fire, but she was a respectable mother of a ten-year-old boy. It wasn't just her anymore.

"You work at a spa?"

One cup and she'd kick him out. Lily glanced over her shoulder at him as he walked to the little kitchen table and hung his coat on the back of a chair. Like two thin arrows, twin creases ran down his back from his shoulders to his waistband, pointing to his nice round butt in those horrible pants.

"I own a spa in Amarillo." She returned her attention to the coffee maker and filled the carafe with water, then poured it into the machine. Not just any guy could make those pants look good. She hit the On button then turned to face him. "Lily Belle Salon and Spa." He picked up an extra teal-and-white invitation from a small stack sitting on the table. "I'm having a big event Saturday. You should come by and win a facial," she joked.

"I don't even really know what that is." He set the invitation back on the table. "Belle is your middle name?"

"Yeah. My mom named my sister and me after flowers."

"It's pretty."

Behind her, the coffeepot spit to life, filling the air with coffee-scented steam. In front of her, Tucker moved across the kitchen. Matching shirt creases ran from the dark brown epaulets on his broad shoulders, slipped beneath his gold star, name bar, and breast pockets. Her gaze followed the thin lines down to his flat belly and further. "Where's your"—she pointed at her waist and then his—"cop stuff?"

"My duty belt?"

"Yeah." She looked back up into his brown eyes. "Your weapons and cuffs?"

"Secured in my truck." His gaze locked with hers and he didn't even bother to hide the interest in his eyes. It was hot and intense, flaming the friction in the pit of her stomach and scattering it across her body. "How long have you had your own spa?"

"Three years." She moved to her left and turned away from his gaze. Away from the chaos it caused, and she opened the cupboard. A collection of random mugs sat inside and she grabbed two. "Do you want cream or sugar?" One cup. Just one cup. She turned and almost hit him in the chest with the pink sparkly Deeann's Duds mug.

"Both." He took the mugs from her and set them on the counter by her hip. "But not in my coffee." He took her hands in his and slid her palms up his chest. "Touch me," he said, his voice a bold rumble beneath her hand.

She raised her gaze from their hands on his breast pockets to his eyes. Suddenly, she couldn't swallow or breathe. He was dangerous and she pulled her hands from beneath his. Cool air hit her heated palms and she closed her fingers into fists.

"Please, Lily." The silent longing in his voice whispered to the dormant longing in her soul. He lowered his face and her breath rushed out.

"What are you doing?" she murmured as his warm mouth skimmed her jaw. "I don't think this is a good idea."

"Then don't think." His warm breath spread across her skin. "I know I have a hard time thinking when I'm near you." He kissed her just beneath her ear.

"Don't say that."

"Why?"

"You don't know me."

"Let's change that." He opened his mouth on her sensitive skin. "Around you, I have a hard time doing anything but getting hard."

"Too soon. That's crude." Her head fell to one side.

"That's the truth. Do you want me to lie?"

Too fast. No. She sometimes liked crude but she knew she shouldn't. She knew she shouldn't let him kiss her throat. She should make him stop, but she couldn't.

"Put your hands on me," he said against her throat and she opened her fingers and slid her hands up to his chest and shoulders. At the touch of her palms on his bare neck, a shudder ran up his spine. "That's good." His mouth slid across her cheek to her lips.

Was this happening? Was she going to let this happen? Right there in her kitchen? Where she cooked breakfast for her son. One of his hands moved to the nape of her neck and tilted her head back with his strong fingers, coaxing her mouth with the promise of a kiss. A warm shiver ran up her spine and he lifted his head. His lips teased her, and she raised onto the balls of her feet and followed his mouth. Evidently she was going to let it happen. Right there in her kitchen where she cooked Eggos and Toaster Sticks.

Beneath the slight pressure of his lips, her mouth opened beneath his and his tongue swept inside. Hot and liquid and unraveling a ribbon of fire from her throat, down her chest to the waiting friction in the pit of her stomach.

He fit his free hand into the curve of her waist and pulled her into him. Her breasts brushed his chest and the kiss deepened. His tongue touched hers while his mouth created a warm suction that felt ripe and so delicious—the ribbon of fire in her stomach engulfed her thighs and tightened her nipples against the front of his shirt.

A deep groan vibrated his chest against her breasts. His grasp on her waist tightened, relaxed, flexed, then slid to her behind. Pleasure flushed her skin and she opened her mouth wider, kissing him deeper. She ran her hands over his shoulders and chest and neck. He untangled his fingers from her hair and slid his palm down the side of her throat and across her shoulder. While his tongue plunged into her mouth, his hand moved to her ribs. He fanned his thumb across Spandex and the side of her breast. Back and forth, driving her mad with the want of his touch. Her breasts tightened while other places in her body turned liquid with need. She melted into him even more. Against her pelvis she felt the stiff ridge of his erection and she rocked against him, loving the feel of it. The size and weight and hard length.

His hands slid to her back, his fingers brushing her bare skin above her tank top. This had to stop, but she didn't want it to. Not now. Now she wanted more. This was crazy. She was crazy. As crazy as everyone said. Crazy Lily lusting after her neighbor and she didn't seem to care. He'd ignited something in her she hadn't felt in a long time. Crazy, consuming lust.

Tucker took a stop back and grasped her shoulders. Her hands slid to down his shirt, his star cool against her palm and his breathing, heavy, harsh, lifting his chest. "Lily. I want more."

Great. She wanted more too. She took a step toward him but his grasp tightened, keeping her at arm's length. She didn't understand. If he wanted more, why was he pushing her away? "So do I," she said, although she thought it was obvious.

"I want you." He dipped his head and his heavy gaze looked into her. "All of you."

She raised a hand to her mouth and touched her wet, tingling lips. Was he talking some strange sexual position? If so, she might be okay with it. Would probably be okay with just about anything. Had probably been there and done that. Several times. But he was young and she had eight years of experience on him. That was probably his attraction to her. "What exactly do you want?" However, there was one part of her that would always remain virgin territory. She didn't judge women who went there. She just wasn't one of them.

"When I saw you today, I knew I wanted every bit of you. That I want to know all of you."

She dropped her hands to her sides. "You said that." She really didn't want to have to come right out and say it but . . . best to be up front because real ladies didn't do it in the back. "My bottom is a no landing strip."

His brows pulled together over his suddenly sharp brown eyes. "What?"

"I just thought you should know."

"Thanks for clearing that up." He frowned and took another step back. "Jesus, Lily. You thought I want anal sex?"

She shook her head, more confused by him than ever before. And he was plenty confusing. She put her hands on top of her head and blew out a breath.

"That's not only disturbing, but insulting."

"I'm disturbing?" She put one palm on her chest. "You said you wanted to know every bit of me. And that bit of me is off limits."

"I wasn't talking about your ass, for Christ sake." He raised a hand, palm up. "I was talking about you. Your life. Your heart and soul."

Her heart and soul?

"I want more than sex."

She turned and grabbed the mugs for something to do with her hands. What could he possibly want? More than sex? All men wanted sex. Her heart and soul? She reached for the coffee carafe and poured. What did that mean?

"I've had relationships that were just about sex. I don't want that anymore. I don't want that with you."

"Relationship?" The coffee sloshed over one side of the Everything's Bigger In Texas mug and she turned to face him.

"Pushing you away was the hardest thing I've ever done." He scrubbed his face with his hands then dropped them to his sides. "I still can't believe I did it, but I don't want to start out that way."

"Start? We can't start anything. We can't have a relationship."

"Why?"

"Because."

"That's not a reason."

"Okay." She raised a hand toward him. "You're thirty and I'm thirty-eight."

"So."

"So I have a young son." She dropped her hand. "I can't just . . . just can't go around . . . with you."

"Because I'm thirty?"

She'd already lived so much down. "People will talk." And it was nice walking into a room and not hearing whispers behind her back.

"So what?"

If he could say that, then people had never talked about him. "They'll say I'm a cougar, and that you must want someone to take care of you."

"Bullshit." He moved across the kitchen and grabbed his coat. "You're not old enough to be a cougar." He shoved his arms into the sleeves. "I have my own house and car and money. I don't need a woman to take care of me. I can take care of myself and anyone else in my life." He stormed across the kitchen but paused in the doorway long enough to say, "I tried to do the right thing today, but the next time I get my hands on you, we're not going to stop." She heard him walk through the living room and open the front door. Then, "Hello Mrs. Brooks."

Crap! Her mom.

"Deputy Matthews?" Lily raised a hand to her throat as her mouth fell open. Please God, just let her mom walk inside without stopping to ramble. "How's your cat?" Obviously God wasn't listening to Lily Darlington. Probably punishing her for putting her hands on the young neighbor.

"Pinky's good. Thanks for asking."

"Marylyle Jeffers had a black cat like yours. She had diabetes and had to have her foot cut off." No wonder Lily acted a bit imprudent sometimes. Her mother was one taco short of a combo plate. "Leg too."

"Oh I'm sorry—"

"Then she caught the pleurisy and died. Not saying it was her cat, but she did have horrible luck. Even before she was struck with—"

"Momma, you're letting out the bought air," Lily interrupted and stuck her head into the living room. She couldn't look at Tucker and pinned her gaze squarely on her mother's pile of gray hair. She was sure she was a bright red and didn't know what was more embarrassing—what she'd done with Tucker or her mother's inane rambling. "Thank you again for carrying in my groceries, Deputy Matthews."

"You're welcome. See you two ladies around."

Louella Brooks stared at the closed door, then turned her gaze to her youngest daughter. "Well."

That one word packed a wealth of meaning. Lily ducked back into the kitchen, looked at the two coffee mugs, and raised the Everything's Bigger In Texas mug to her mouth. She managed to hammer back half. It burned her tongue and throat and she set it back down as her mother entered the room.

"He certainly is a nice-looking boy."

Lily swallowed past her scalded taste buds and throat. She reached for her pink Deeann's Duds mug and turned with a slight smile on her face. "Nice too. He carried in my groceries."

A scowl settled into the wrinkles on her mother's face. "You're a single woman, Lily. You have to be careful who you let in your house."

"He's a deputy. What do you think he's going to do? Kill me? Touch me? Kiss me? Drive me as crazy as everyone says I am?

"I wasn't talking about your physical safety."

Lily knew that. "He just carried in my groceries and had a half a cup of coffee." With her free hand, she pointed to the mug on the counter. "Then he left." And thank God too. If he hadn't stopped when he had, her mother would have used her key and strolled inside. The mere thought of her mother walking in on her and Tucker was too horrible to contemplate.

"Single gals can't be too careful when it comes to their reputations. Just the other day, the cable repairman was in Doreen Jaworski's house for three hours." She gave Lily a knowing look. "Cable repairs don't take three hours."

"Ma, Doreen is in her seventies."

"Exactly. She always did wear her clothes kind of sudden. Or course that was before she married Lynn Jaworski . . . which just goes to show, people's memories are longer than pulled taffy."

Lily closed her eyes and blew into her coffee.

"Her daughter Dorlynn didn't fall far from that tree. She—"

Lily didn't bother to stop her mother. Louella was going to talk until she ran out of words, which could take a while. Since her mother's retirement from the Wild Coyote Diner, the rambling had gotten worse. Nothing to do for it but block out her mother's voice and retreat into her own head. Unfortunately, her head was filled with Tucker. He'd said he wanted a relationship, but he didn't know her. Didn't know her past and what everyone said about her. At least not yet. He'd no doubt change his mind once she heard about the Ronnie incident of '04.

Lily took a sip of coffee and winched as it hit her scalded tongue. But her past wasn't the biggest reason any sort of relationship was impossible. She was busy. She didn't have time. She couldn't get involved with him.

He was thirty. She hadn't even known what she'd wanted at thirty.

He might not have a problem with the age difference, but she did. People would call her a cougar. That crazy cougar, Lily Darlington. If it was just about her, she might risk it. Might show the world her middle finger. But it wasn't just her. She'd gone to school with a momma who wasn't wound too tight. Kids could be really cruel, and she couldn't do that to Pip.

Chapter Five

The rows of track lighting in Lily Belle's Salon and Day Spa sparkled like gold fire in the sequins of the owner's dress. The long-sleeved dress covered Lily from collar bone to mid-thigh, and might have been considered modest if not for the fact that it clung to the curves of her body. A body she kept thin and toned through a busy life, Rodney Yee, and the Pilates Power Gym in one of the spa's back rooms. She not only cut hair, she was the owner and face of her business, and it was important that she reflect a positive, healthy image.

Lily's blond hair was pulled into a loose, sexy bun on the left side of her head, and she stood in the middle of the spa, chatting and sipping her first glass of champagne of the night. The party was officially over in half an hour and she was looking forward to slipping her feet out of the sparkly gold pumps. The spa had given away over ten thousand dollars in products and services and signed up a lot of clients for spa packages. Given the expense of the party and giveaways, Lily figured she'd broken even, which was fine with her. Her goal had been to bring in new clients, make them happy so they'd return. And with each return visit, happy clients generally wanted to try the newest facial or latest filler.

"I need to get going," her sister, Daisy, said as she moved toward Lily. She wove her arms through her tan trench coat and pulled her blond hair from beneath the collar. Daisy was six months pregnant and a red maternity dress hugged her belly. Daisy was older, but Lily was taller. There were other little differences between the two, but they looked enough alike that there was no denying they were sisters.

"I'll walk you out."

"No need."

"I want to." Lily set her glass on a table and moved through the spa toward the front. "I'm so glad you came tonight."

"I didn't win a darn thing, though."

Lily smiled and opened the door. "Don't worry about it. I know the owner and I'll hook you up."

"Good, 'cause once this baby is born, I need some color in my hair and Botox in my forehead."

Lily folded her arms across her chest and huddled against the chill of the night. "I've been trying to talk mom into getting Dysport because she doesn't want 'poison' in her face."

Daisy laughed. "How did it go with Ronnie yesterday?"

Lily shrugged as the two moved across the parking lot. Their heels tapping against the pavement as they walked to Daisy's new van. "Ronnie was an hour late, of course. But he did make it."

"Do we think that's progress?"

Lily shook her head and a gold hoop earring brushed her neck. "We think it's a fluke. He's dumber than a road lizard and admitted his last girlfriend took off with his big screen

TV and Xbox. Once he finds a new sloozy, he'll forget about Pippen again."

"Oh, my gosh," Daisy said, disgust lowering her voice. "He still plays Xbox? At his age? What a loser."

"I know. Right?" Lily laughed. "A thirty-eight-year-old 'gamer.' He probably sits around with one hand on the controller and the other on his balls."

"Ick."

"It's just embarrassing that I ever married him."

"Well, at least Pippen takes after you." An awkward pause stretched between them before Daisy said, "You had a hard time for a while, but you came though all that. And look at you now." They stopped by the van and Daisy opened the driver's side door. "I'm really proud of you, Lil."

Her heart got all mushy. "Thanks."

"And I wanted to ask you if it would be okay if we name the baby after you."

Her mushy heart got all tingly and the backs of her eyes pinched. "Are you sure?"

"Absolutely."

"Is Jack sure?" Given her past, it might be something the baby had to live down.

"It was originally his idea, but as soon as he mentioned it, I knew I wanted to name her Lily too. It just seems right, but I wanted to make sure you weren't planning on having your own baby 'Lily' someday."

Lily laughed. "I don't even have a boyfriend." For some weird reason Tucker's face popped into her head. "And I don't see a man in my future. I don't think I have very good judgment."

"The rat bastard doesn't count. He never deserved you, and you deserve someone as great as you, Lily. Someone who looks at you and knows he's lucky."

Someone like Jack. Jack looked at Daisy like that. She hugged her sister. "You're going to make my face run." She stepped back and waved her hands in front of her eyes.

Daisy climbed into the van. "Go back inside before you catch your death."

"Drive carefully and take good care of little Lily." She took a step back as Daisy fired up the engine, then waved as her sister pulled out of the parking lot. She refolded her arms and smiled as she walked toward the front of the spa. *Little Lily.* Several years ago, she had given up the dream of finding the right man and giving Pip a sibling. She'd always wanted a happy family, and hoped for two kids and a dog, but it just wasn't in the cards for her. That was okay. Her family wasn't perfect, but they were happy.

When she opened the door to her salon, she had a big grin on her face. There had been a time when she and Daisy hadn't been very close, and now she was naming her baby girl after her. *Little Lily.*

While she'd been outside with Daisy, the rest of the clients had left and only a few employees remained. The sound of female laughter filled the front of the spa and salon as the caterers started to pack up and break tables down—laughter mixed with one deeper chuckle. Lily's feet skidded to a halt and her gaze took in the back of a familiar dark head, broad shoulders narrowing to a trim waist and nice behind. She didn't need to see a uniform or ratty sweatshirt to recognize Tucker Matthews.

"Deputy Matthews."

"Hey, Lily." He turned toward her and his brown eyes took her in with one sweeping glance. "You said to come by and get a facial."

She looked at the faces looking back at her. At the inquisitive gazes of her assistant manager, two beauticians, and aesthetician. "Deputy Matthews is my neighbor and I mentioned he should come by and *win* a facial." She turned toward him. "I didn't think you'd take me up on it."

"Yeah. I noticed there aren't any men here tonight."

A few women had dragged their husbands or boyfriends, but they'd left as soon as the final prize had been won. She glanced at the clock on the wall above a manicure station. "The party is over in fifteen minutes. If you wanted to win a facial you're too late."

His grin told her he knew that. "You should show me around your salon. In case I need"—he glanced around—"a haircut or something."

No, she *shouldn't*. The caterer caught her attention and gave her a nod. "I have a few checks to write," she said. "Maybe one of the girls will show you."

"I will," young, perky Melinda Hartley volunteered.

Tucker lifted one brow and wrinkled the scar on his forehead.

"Excuse me." Lily moved through the salon to her office. The caterer followed her. She sat down at a desk covered in paperwork and a big open appointment book; her computer sat at one end of the desk, and behind it hung a massive ornate mirror that had once decorated a brothel in Tascosa. The caterer sat opposite, slid a red velvet chair toward Lily's big

desk, and then they went over the bill. While they counted
the bottles of wine and champagne that had been consumed
and calculated the charges for the extra linen Lily had or-
dered at the last minute, her mind was elsewhere in the salon.
Melinda Hartley was about twenty-five. She was pretty and a
really good colorist. She was also a little conceited and loud.
If Melinda was in the room, everyone knew it. Just as everyone knew all about Melinda's sex life, whether they wanted to
know or not. She *was* a butt girl, and Lily had had to talk to
her about appropriate workplace conversation. If it wasn't for
the fact that it was hard to find a good colorist in the Texas
panhandle, she would have fired Melinda months ago.

And she was out there. In the salon. Somewhere with
Tucker. Probably telling him about her sex life. Tucker was a
guy. He was probably loving it.

Lily wrote out the balance she owed the caterer and tore
the check from her business account. She handed it across
her desk and watched the caterer walk out the door. Melinda
was closer to Tucker's age and didn't have a child and Lily's
baggage. She shuffled the paperwork on her desk, sorting cus-
tomer surveys and treatment plans. Until tonight, she hadn't
seen Tucker since that morning in her kitchen five days ago.
She'd heard from Pippen that the two played basketball
when Pip got home from school and before Tucker got ready
for work. By the time Lily made it home, Tucker was already
gone, which was a good thing. He clearly wasn't good for her
good intentions.

"Now, that wasn't very nice."

Lily glanced up at Tucker leaning a shoulder into the
doorframe of her office. He wore a gray crew neck sweater

and button-fly Levi's. His arms were crossed over his chest and he looked annoyed—annoyed and good enough to nibble up one side and down the other. "What?"

"Melinda."

She rose from her chair and moved to the front of her desk. "You didn't like her?"

He shrugged one shoulder. "Not really. She's loud and talks too much." He pushed away from where he was leaning and shut the door. "She wanted me to screw her on a massage table."

That was a bit crude and she'd get to his language in a minute. The inappropriateness of shutting the door too, but first she wanted to know . . . "Did she say that?"

"Not exactly. She was much more graphic about where she wanted it."

"Oh." Lily moved past the red chair to the center of her desk and sat on the edge. "She can say really inappropriate and offensive things. She's one of those people who doesn't have a filter, but I didn't know she'd go that far."

He shrugged. "I wasn't offended. I was in the Army for ten years, I've heard worse."

She took a breath and let it out. "Thank you for not taking her up on her offer in the massage room."

He moved toward Lily. "She isn't the woman I want to shove on a table." He stopped in front of her and she stood so she wouldn't have to stare up at him. Just a few sequins separated his chest from hers. "Isn't her panties I want to see around her ankles." He took her hand and slid it up his chest. "You're the women I want to shove on a table with your panties around your ankles."

"Tucker! Don't say things like that."

"Why not?" He buried his fingers in her loose bun on the side of her head. "It's the truth. I told you how I feel about you. I want you. I want everything about you. Getting you naked is one of the things I want." With her four-inch heels, they were close to the same height and he pressed his forehead into hers. "I know you want that too."

After the other morning, she couldn't exactly deny it, and she was too old to play coy games. "Anyone can walk in here." The fire he'd started in her veins a few days ago flared in her chest. The crazy consuming lust that absolutely could not happen here.

He shook his head and his eyes turned a shade darker. "They had their coats on and were walking outside when I came in here."

"They could come back."

"I locked the door."

"We can't do this here." She meant to sound more forceful, but the crazy, consuming lust burned her throat and toasted her pitiful resistance.

"That's what I thought until you stood up and walked toward me. You shouldn't have worn that dress."

"You're blaming my dress?" But this is Amarillo, she rationalized. Not Lovett. In a town the size of Lovett, the fact that he'd shown up tonight would have been telegraphed to half the town by now. In Amarillo, she was just another salon owner and no one cared.

"Yes, and the tight outfit you had on Monday. The way you've been in my head for the past five days and the hard-on that won't go away no matter how many times I abuse myself.

I didn't think we were going to do this here, but I'm think we have to now."

"What if someone—" His mouth on hers silenced her protest. The other morning, he'd started slower, kissing her neck and throat and cheek. Easing her into it. Tonight he hit her fast with hot lust and wet pleasure. His mouth working hers, feeding and hungry. It pulled her up on her toes and smashed her against his chest, so close she could feel the pounding of his heart. Her hands slid over his arms and shoulders and the back of his head. And like the other morning, a deep shuddering groan vibrated in his chest as if he couldn't get enough of her touch. She liked knowing she did that to him. A strong beautiful man who couldn't get enough of Lily Darlington.

She kissed him back, her tongue slick with carnal implications. He pressed his erection into her pelvis and she had to lock her knees to keep from falling. She slid up his chest then back down, feeling every hard muscle and length of his harder erection.

He grasped the bottom of her sequined dress, drew it up her thighs to her waist. His hands found her bare behind and he fingered the thin lace of her thong panties. He palmed her bare backside and rubbed his denim button fly against the tiny triangle of lace covering her crotch.

He lifted his face and came up for air. "Lily," he gasped.

She looked into his eyes, dark and sleepy with lust, and reached for the bottom of his sweater. She pulled it over his head and tossed it to the wooden floor. She lowered her gaze to the brown hair on his hard, defined chest. For some reason, she'd thought his chest would be bare. But it wasn't. He was a man with a man's chest and a thin line of hair trailed down his flat abdomen, circled his navel, and darted beneath the waist-band of his Levi's. A snarling bulldog was tattooed on the ball of his shoulders with the words U.S. ARMY inked beneath. RELENTLESS was tattooed in heavy black ink on the inside of his forearm, which described him perfectly: his hands, his mouth, and the lust rolling off him in heavy, relentless waves.

She bent forward and kissed his shoulder, ran her fingers across his pec and down his belly to the front of his jeans. She squeezed his erection and caressed him through the denim. Desire, hot and gripping, tightened her breasts and stomach and pulled between her legs.

"Wait." He grabbed her shoulders and turned her until her back was against his chest. He reached for the zipper on the back of her dress and slid it down. Through the old bordello mirror, she watched as he slid her dress from her shoulders. Just before it slipped down her arms, she placed her hands on the sequins over her breasts.

"I have implants," she told him. She hadn't worn a bra because strap lines showed beneath the tight dress, and in a moment he would see the thin scars beneath each areola.

Confusion lowered his brows. "What?"

"I have breast implants. Do you have a problem with that?"

"Is that a trick question?"

She shook her head as he grasped her wrists. "Some men don't like implants."

In the mirror, he raised his gaze from her hands to her face. "A man told you that?"

She shook her head. "A few women in my chair over the years have mentioned it."

"A man would never say that unless he thought it would get him laid." He shoved her wrists to her sides. For a second, her dress caught on her hard nipples then slid down her stomach to her waist. "Lily." The breath left his lungs and brushed the side of her head. "You're beautiful."

The dress fell to the floor and she kicked it aside. She stood in front of the mirror wearing nothing but her white panties—owning a salon and spa made it easy for her to keep her pubic area waxed and trimmed into a perfect triangle hidden beneath her thong—but looking at her abdomen . . . it was flat but not as tight and toned as she'd like. She examined the palm-size yellow-and-orange lily tattoo on the inside of her hip that she'd thought was such a good idea six years ago. "Are you lying to get laid?" She tried to turn to face him, away from her image in the mirror, but his hands moved to her abdomen and he pulled her against him. The hair on his chest tickled her bare back. She felt completely wrapped up, surrounded by his relentless passion.

"I'll never lie to you, Lily." He slid one hand up and cupped her breast. Her hard nipple stabbed his warm palm and her breath caught in her lungs. "You're so beautiful and I ache to be with you."

She knew the feeling. She ached too. All over. Then he slipped his hand beneath the little triangle of her thong and touched her where she ached most.

"You're wet," he whispered next to her ear. "Push your panties down for me. Push 'em down around your ankles." He brushed this thumb across her nipple and again she had to lock her knees to keep from sliding to the floor. She did as he asked, then looked at his big hands—one covering her breast the other her crotch. He slid his fingers deeper between her thighs and she reached behind her bare bottom and slipped her own hand beneath the waistband of his jeans. She wrapped her hand around his hot thick shaft and squeezed. She reached up with her free hand and brought his mouth down to hers. She gave him a long wet kiss and her heart pounded in her chest. She loved the way he touched her. She wanted him every bit as much as he wanted her.

Tucker lifted his mouth from Lily's and looked into the deep blue of her heavily lidded eyes. He turned his attention to the mirror and watched his hands on her body . . . on the perfect patch between her legs, and his fingers lightly pinching her pink nipples. Her hand gripping his cock was driving him close to the edge. She tore at the buttons of his Levi's, and he pulled a condom from his back pocket a second before his pants slid down his legs.

"Grab the desk with your hands."

She stepped one foot out of her thong, the she bent foreword and looked back over her shoulder at him. "You remember the no man's land, right?"

"I'll never do anything you're not comfortable doing." He didn't want to hurt her. He wanted to make it so good she wanted more. He pulled himself out of his boxer-briefs and rolled the condom down t shaft of his penis. "Spread your feet a little bit for me."

She did and he slid his hand over her bottom and between her legs. She was wet and ready and he parted her slick flesh. Her back arched as he positioned himself and he slid into the hot pleasure of her body. She was incredibly tight around him. Pulling him deeper and deeper until he couldn't sink any deeper.

She moaned low in her throat and whispered his name. He looked in the mirror, at him naked behind her, her beautiful face turned back, looking at him. *Mine,* he thought as he pulled out and thrust into her again. She pushed her bottom against him. Straining, wanting more. He gave it to her in long powerful thrusts. He drove inside again and again, his heart pounded *boom-boom-boom*. *Mine. Mine. Mine.* Over the roar in his head and ears, he heard her say his name. Telling him she wanted him. More. Harder.

"Tucker," she moaned loud enough to be heard in the next county as he felt the first tightening pulse of her orgasm. Good, he thought on some primal level. He was sure they were the only two left in the salon, but he didn't care. If there was anyone around, they'd know what the two of them were doing. Know they were together. That she belonged to him now. He'd never been a possessive man, but as her orgasm pulled his own release from deep in his belly, he knew that he wanted this to last forever.

The most intense pleasure he'd ever felt in his life rippled through his body and slammed into his heart. It spread fire across his skin, grabbed his insides, and stole his breath. He doubled over and planted his hands on the desk next to Lily's. He buried his face in the curve of her neck and closed his eyes.

As crazy as it sounded . . . as crazy as it felt . . . as crazy as it was—he'd fallen in love with her even before he'd walked into her salon earlier. He'd fallen for her that first day in her driveway.

"Jesus," he whispered. He'd never fallen so fast and hard

and it scared the hell out of him. Scared him more than Taliban rounds whizzing past his nose and slamming into the granite mountain by his left ear. He'd been trained by the military what to do in combat. Trained by the sheriff's department how to take down a felon bent on escape. But this? This was new territory. There was no training. No taking cover. No fighting back. There was just Lily and how she made him feel.

CHAPTER SIX

Monday morning, Lily pulled her Jeep into the parking lot of Crockett Elementary School and reached into the backseat. "My last appointment is at four. It's just a cut and style so I should be home around six." She stopped the SUV next to the sidewalk and handed Pippen his Angry Birds backpack. "What do you want for dinner?"

He wore his red coat zipped all the way to his chin and said into the nylon collar, "Pizza."

Of course. She leaned toward him. "Give me some sugar, sugar."

He unbuckled himself. "Tonight," he said. He'd stopped giving her sugar at school last year, but a mom could always try. "Is Tucker coming to play basketball today?"

She shrugged. "He's working, so I don't know. I haven't talked to him." Not since he'd left her house yesterday around noon. Only half an hour before Ronnie had dropped Pippen off home. Four hours early, which was so typical of Ronnie. She hadn't been all that surprised. She was just glad she'd been alone and had taken a shower.

Pippen opened the door and slid out of the car. "Maybe he will."

"Maybe." She gave him a little wave. "Love you, Pip."

"Love you, Momma." He shut the door and she watched him run to a group of his friends hanging out near the playground equipment. She took her foot off the brake and drove out of the parking lot. Her first appointment today wasn't until noon. Her assistance manager was certainly capable of running the salon when Lily wasn't there.

She stopped at a red light and thought about the last time she'd been in the salon, having sex with Tucker in her office. Sex that had been so good she might have moaned Tucker's name a little too loud. She hoped she hadn't and that everyone had already left the building like he'd said. By the time they'd redressed and left the office, the salon had been empty. Thank God.

After she'd left the salon that night, Tucker followed her home in his truck and they'd spent the rest of the night in her bed—having sex and talking. At least she'd talked. It seemed like every time she asked him questions about himself, he changed the subject back to her or kissed her until she didn't feel like talking anymore.

She pulled her Jeep into the garage and closed the door. She couldn't exactly be angry about his lack of personal disclosure. There were certain things in her past that she wasn't going to talk about either.

The cell in her purse rang before she even got in the back door. She figured it was someone at the salon and answered without looking at the number. "This is Lily."

"This is your neighbor. Come over so I can kiss you good night."

Lily smiled. "Mom?"

Tucker chuckled and she could see his smile in her head. A smile that curved his lips and lit up his brown eyes. "Come over or I'll come over and get you."

She couldn't have that. Her mother might walk in. "Give me a few minutes." She hung up and changed out of the yoga outfit she'd worn in anticipation of working out. She had a whole different workout in mind now and changed into a pink-and-blue polka dot nighty, pink thong, and pink cowboy boots. She tied her trench coat around her waist and checked her pink lipstick in the mirror.

There were three boards missing at the back of the fence that separated her yard from Tucker's. The previous owner's Newfoundland, Griffin, had always preferred her yard to his; and no matter how many times she'd fixed the boards, Griffin knocked them down whenever he heard Pippen playing outside. Griffin had been a sweetheart of a dog—huge, but a sweetheart who'd had a real fondness for Pip. After about the fifth time of Griffin knocking down the boards, Lily had given up and left them stacked neatly on the ground.

Lily grabbed a pot of coffee on her way out the door.

Tucker had said several times that he wanted her. He wanted everything about her, but he didn't know everything about her. He didn't know her past. He didn't know that people thought she was crazy. At least, she figured if he did know, he would have mentioned it right before he took off running for the hills. She wasn't going to be the one to tell him.

She moved through her yard, slipped through the fence, and knocked on his back door. "Italian roast?" she asked and held up the pot as he answered the door.

His brows pulled over his eyes and his scar wrinkled. "How did you get back here?" He wore a beige cold-weather base layer that clung to his chest and arms like a second skin. And of course his work pants and boots.

"A few boards are missing in the fence."

He held the door open and she stepped inside. "Convenient."

The kitchen was pretty much as she recalled from the last time she'd been in the place, when the realtor had spruced up the place for an open house. Oak cabinets, white walls, new gray counter tops, and vinyl flooring with a stone pattern. A small black cat sat by the door to the garage, lapping up milk from one of two purple bowls with flowers painted around the edges. The bowls sat on a little white rug with the name PINKY written in pink at the bottom.

Lily set the carafe on the counter and reached for her belt. "My mom told me you have a cat."

"Pinky got out and I had to track her down that day I met your mother," Tucker said as he reached into a cupboard and pulled out two plain white mugs. "Pinky has no survival skills."

Lily bit the side of her lip to keep from laughing. "How did you end up with a cat with no survival skills?"

"She belonged to an old girlfriend."

"And she just gave her to you?" Lily shrugged out of her coat, hung it over a chair, and stooped down by the little cat.

"Not exactly. The girlfriend moved out and left her cat behind."

The hem of the nighty slid down her thighs as she lightly stroked the cat from the back of her head to her tail. "She abandoned her animal?" Lily couldn't imagine that. She liked cats but didn't have a pet because she wasn't home enough to take care of one. Now that Griffin was gone, Pippen was harassing her for a dog.

When Tucker didn't answer her question, she looked up over her shoulder at him. He stood in the middle of the room—two mugs of coffee in his hands, like his feet were frozen in place. "What?"

"What are you wearing?"

She stood. "A comfy nighty and my cowboy boots."

"Panties?" He held the mug toward her as his eyes slid over his body.

"No self-respecting Southern lady leaves the house without her hair in place, her makeup done, and her panties on." She took the mug from his hand and blew into it. "That sort of fast behavior could lead to a bad reputation. I went to high school with Francine Holcomb, and she left the house without wearing her undies on more than one occasion. Her reputation never did recover. 'Course, everyone knew that Francie was as loose as grits, bless her heart." She took a sip. She was nervous and had to stop before she sounded like her mother. "How was your day?"

He brought his gaze up to hers. "Better now."

For the first time since she'd stepped in his kitchen, she noticed the pinch of exhaustion at the corners of his brown eyes. "You look tired. Did something happen at work?"

He shrugged a shoulder and leaned his hip into a counter. "I responded to a call about one this morning at Rodale

Jewelry store on Seventh near the highway. When I got there, a guy was trying to kick in the back door. He saw me and took off." He took a swallow of coffee. "I chased him for about half a mile before I caught him climbing inside a Dumpster behind Rick's Bait & Tackle."

Lily wrinkled her nose. "Did you have to climb into the Dumpster?"

"I grabbed his belt just as he was diving in and pulled him back out. It was real ripe too. Smelled like Rick had just thrown out some expired bait. If I'd had to jump in there and get covered with fish eggs and dead crickets, I'd have been pissed."

She couldn't imagine running in work boots and gear. She was in good shape, but probably would have passed out after a hundred feet. "Was he from around here?"

"Odessa." Tucker looked at the scratches across the back of his hand. "He was scrappy for such a skinny guy."

Lily moved toward him and took his hand in hers. "How'd this happen?"

"He didn't want to be cuffed very badly, and I scrapped it on the concrete trying to dig his arm from underneath him."

She raised his hand to her mouth and lightly kissed it. "Better?"

"Yes." He looked back into her eyes and nodded. "He tried to kick me in the balls too."

"I'm not going to kiss your hairy balls, Tucker."

He chuckled like he thought he was real funny. "Didn't hurt to mention it."

She dropped his hand and thought for a moment. "Well, maybe if you got them waxed."

He sucked in a breath through his teeth. "Do men do that?"

"Some men." He looked so horrified it was her turn to chuckle. "They wax their whole bodies. It's called manscaping."

He set his mug on the counter. "No one is going to put hot wax anywhere near my balls." He ran his hands up her arms and pulled her close.

"Don't be a baby." She set her mug on the counter next to his. "I get waxed."

"I noticed." He grinned. "I like it. It makes going down on you real nice and neat. I can see what I'm doing."

Her eyes widened and she felt color creep up her cheeks. "You looked at my . . . my crotch."

"Of course. My face was down there. I don't know why you're embarrassed. You've got a real nice . . ." He paused as if searching for the right word then gave up. "I don't like the word *crotch*. I've got a crotch. You're all high and tight and pretty down there. Like a juicy peach." His brows drew together. "Or is that one of those things I shouldn't say?"

She didn't know. She supposed it was a compliment, but it had been a while since she'd been involved with a man. She couldn't recall if they talked so free and easy in the beginning or if they saved their real thoughts for later—after they reached that comfortable stage. Or was it just Tucker? "Have you always talked this way to women?" Or maybe guys Tucker's age where just more direct.

He looked up toward the ceiling and thought a minute. "No." His gaze returned to hers. "I used to have a filthy mouth. When I was in the Army I talked a lot worse. I had to work really hard to get the f-word out of every sentence. I couldn't even ask for the ketchup without dropping it at least twice. In the military, swearing is not only a way of life, it's an art form." He slid his hands across her shoulders to her neck and his thumbs brushed her chin and jaw. "Living with a bunch of guys for months on end in a bunker in an Afghanistan outpost will turn anyone into an animal. You get shot at every day, live in dirt, and the food's shitty. Inventive swearing is just something to do to pass the time and impress the other guys."

"You must have liked it. You did it for ten years."

"I loved it right up until the second that I didn't."

"What made you decide you didn't love it anymore?" She put her palms on his flat belly and brushed her fingers across the fabric of his shirt. She knew he loved it when she ran her hands all over him. Her touch seemed to soothe even as it excited him. And she loved the feel of his hard muscles and tight skin beneath her hand and mouth.

"The last time I took rounds, I got shot five times. Four were stopped by my ballistic plates." Her fingers stopped and she raised her gaze to where he pointed at the scar on his forehead. "The fifth got me here and I decided I didn't want to be taken out that way. I'd given the Army enough. It was time to do something else. When my enlistment was up, I got out."

She stared at his forehead, horrified. "You could have died, Tucker. I bet your family was worried sick."

"I didn't die and I'm here with you." He kissed her up-turned mouth. "I like having you here when I come home. You should come over every morning."

She settled against his chest. "I can't every morning. I have to work."

"What time do you work today?"

"I have to be there by noon."

He raised the big watch on his wrist. "Then why are we out here wasting time?" He reached for her hand, led her out of the kitchen, and through the living room. She got a quick impression of wood and leather and real art on the walls—no nudie posters or dogs playing poker painted on velvet. He had a big screen TV and books. They continued down the hall and she looked in a bathroom that appeared surprisingly clean. She hadn't known what to expect, but not this. Not this grown-up house, with big-boy furniture. It just didn't fit her preconceived image of him. "Do you play Xbox?"

"I'm thirty, not thirteen." He stopped next to a bed with a real headboard. "I'm only too glad to show you I'm a grown man. Although, after our sexual three-peat the other night, I'm surprised it's even in question."

During the next few weeks, Lily snuck through the back fence several more times after she took Pippen to school. There were some women, she supposed, who would have qualms about sneaking around. That would feel uneasy or guilty or that she was doing something wrong. Lily wasn't one of them. She liked Tucker. She liked spending time with him. She was wildly attracted to him and he made her laugh. He seemed to have his head on straight and he was good to her son. He was also very good in bed, and she didn't want to stop sneaking through the fence to spend time with him.

The more time she spent with him, the more she discovered things about him. Like that Tucker recycled old wood. He made a coffee table out of an old door and a chair and his entertainment center out of wood he'd reclaimed from a demolished ranch house near Houston. She also learned that he ran five miles on a treadmill and lifted weights, which was good because he liked a big breakfast before he went to bed in the morning.

While he ate, she sipped coffee and answered questions he asked about her life. He himself gave up little about his own, though. He talked about his job and who he'd arrested and on what charge, and he talked about playing basketball with Pippen while she was at work. He talked a little about the men who'd served with him in the Army and his time in Iraq and Afghanistan. He said that after he got out of the Army, he was closed off but wasn't anymore. For a guy who didn't consider himself "closed off," he would only go so deep into his life, and when she asked about his family, he told her they were all dead. Case closed. End of story.

Conversely, he asked a lot of questions about her family, and like him, she only went so deep. She told him about growing up in such a small town and that she'd fallen for Rat Bastard Ronnie Darlington because Ronnie owned a truck and looked good in a pair of jeans and a T-shirt. She talked about her low expectations and lower self-esteem. She talked about Ronnie leaving her with a two-year-old and a drained bank account, but didn't mention the part about driving her car into his house.

On the third Monday they both had off, she told him about the time her sister Daisy had tried to kick Ronnie in the crotch outside the Minute Mart. Of course, she didn't mention that she'd been involved in a hair-pulling fight with Kelly the Skank at the same time. Let him think Daisy, the responsible one, was the crazy sister.

They spent the next few hours in bed, and when she got up and dressed he stacked his hands behind his head and watched her.

"When are you going to come to my front door?" he asked.

She looked across her shoulder at him as she hooked her bra behind her back. "I can't do that." She'd been the subject of gossip and speculative gazes most of her life, but she hadn't given the people of Lovett anything to talk about in a long time. She planned to keep it that way. "People will talk."

"Who cares?"

She reached for her blouse and threaded her arms though the sleeves. "I do. I'm a single mother." She pulled her hair from beneath the collar. "I have to be careful." And if and when their relationship ended, no one would know about it. She'd probably be upset. It would be awkward, but the whole town wouldn't know she'd been dumped again—this time by a younger man. She could hold her head up, and Pippen wouldn't have to live it down.

Tucker sat up and swung his feet over the side of the bed. He watched her button up the front and he stood and stepped into a pair of jeans. He loved opening his back door and seeing here there, but he wanted more. "There's a difference between being careful and thinking we need to keep a dirty secret."

She glanced up from her hands. "I don't think we're a dirty secret." A secret, yes. Dirty, no.

"Have you told your sister about me?" He arranged his junk then zipped up his pants. "Your mother? Anyone?"

Her blond hair brushed her cheeks as she shook her head. "Why is it anyone's business?"

"Because we're sneaking around like we're doing something wrong and we're not." He reached for a T-shirt and pulled it over his head. "I told you right up front I want all of you. I'm not going to treat you like you're just a piece of ass."

"I appreciate that, Tucker." She stepped into a pair of black pants. "But I have a ten-year-old son and I have to be very careful."

"I like Pippen. I'd play ball with him even if you weren't in the picture. He's a funny little kid, and I think he likes me."

"He does."

"I would never do anything to hurt him."

She looked up at him as she buttoned her pants. "Kids are cruel. I don't want our relationship to be something that Pippen has to hear about at school."

More than anyone, he knew how mean kids could be. "Duly noted." But it was more than Pippen. Tucker might be younger than Lily, but that didn't mean he'd been born yesterday. For some reason, Lily wanted to keep their relationship a secret for reasons other than her son. Tucker wanted to get a megaphone and let the whole town know. This feeling was new to him. He'd been in love before, but never like this. Never fallen this hard—so hard he wanted to put his hands on her shoulders and shake her even as he wanted to pull her into his chest and keep her there forever.

This situation was new to him. She had a son. He had to be careful of Pippen's feelings, but that didn't mean he was going to hide like he was doing something wrong. As if Lily had to live like a nun and they had to sneak around like sinners. He'd be respectful, but he wasn't anyone's secret and sneaking around just wasn't his style.

CHAPTER SEVEN

"My mama worked at the Wild Coyote Diner until she retired last year," Lily said as she painted vanilla crème and butterscotch highlights into her eleven-thirty appointment's hair. For dimension, she added a caramel lowlight every third foil. With the tail of her brush, she sectioned off a thin line, wove the tail through the strands, then she slid a foil next to her client's scalp. "And my brother-in-law owns Parrish American Classics."

"I used to eat at the Wild Coyote all the time. Open-face sandwiches and pecan pie." Wrapped in a black salon cape, her client, Sadie Hollowell, looked back at her through the mirror. "What's your mama's name?"

"Louella Brooks."

"Of course, I remember her," Sadie said. And Lily remembered Sadie Hollowell. Sadie was several years younger than Lily, but everyone knew the Hollowells. They owned the JH Ranch and had run cattle in the panhandle for generations. And if there was one person the people in town loved to talk about more than Lily, it was anyone with the last name Hollowell. Sadie had moved away from Lovett for a good number of years, but she was back now taking care of her sick daddy. Being that she was the very last Hollowell, Sadie was numero uno with the Lovett gossips. You couldn't swing a cat without hitting someone who was talking about Sadie.

Just yesterday, Lily had cut Winnie Stokes's hair and heard that Sadie had left the Founder's Day celebration last Saturday with Luraleen Jink's nephew, Vince Haven. According to Winnie, Vince was the new owner of the Gas and Go and a former Navy SEAL. Supposedly, he was hotter than a pepper patch and his truck had been spotted at the Hollowell ranch house well into the wee hours of the morning. Evidently, Sadie didn't care if people gossiped about her or she would have made Vince hide his truck in the barn. Lily envied Sadie that screw-you-all attitude. Maybe if she ever moved away like Sadie, she'd have it too.

A bell above the door chimed, and through the mirror a huge bouquet of red roses entered the salon, so big it hid the delivery man. "Oh, no." He set the flowers on the front counter and one of the girls signed for them.

"Are those for you?" Sadie asked.

"I'm afraid so." Yesterday Tucker had sent stargazer lilies. His way of letting her know that he would not sneak around. He wasn't hiding.

"That's sweet."

"No, it's not. He's too young for me," she said and felt a blush creep up her neck. Everyone in the salon knew about Tucker. After he'd showed up at the spa party, and locked the door to her office, there was little doubt what Lily Darlington was doing with the young Deputy Matthews. Adding to the intrigue and gossip was the fact that she arrived late some-times to the salon. Before Tucker, she'd always been one of the first to arrive.

She painted strands of hair, then wrapped the foil. Salons filled with female employees were just a natural hotbed of gossip, and Lily's salon was buzzing more than usual. She had to do something. Something to make it stop before it reached Lovett. But other than kicking Tucker out of her life, she didn't know what to do about it. Telling everyone to shut the hell up would only confirm it.

"How old is he?"

She sectioned off another slice of hair. "Thirty."

"That's only eight years, right?"

"Yeah, but I don't want to be a cougar." God, she hated even the thought of that word. So far the gossip had been con-tained to the salon here in Amarillo, but it was only a matter of time before it spread to Lovett. She shouldn't have had sex with Tucker in her office. For a woman who cared about gossip, that had clearly been a mistake. One she should regret perhaps more than she did.

"You don't look like a cougar."

She didn't feel like one either. "Thanks." She slid a foil against Sadie's scalp. "He looks about twenty-five."

"I think he has to be young enough to be your son before it's considered a cougar-cub relationship."

"Well, I don't want to date a man eight years younger." She swiped color out of one of the bowls and continued painting Sadie's hair. No, she didn't want to date someone eight years younger, but she didn't want to stop seeing Tucker either. Just the thought of him gave her that funny, scary feeling in her stomach and made her heart hurt in her chest. Her feelings for him scared her. Scared her in a way she hadn't been scared in a long time. "But Lordy, he's hot." And smart and funny and nice. He'd built Pinky a cat condo, for goodness sakes.

"Just use him for his body."

"I tried that." She sighed, thinking about the flowers and his suggestion yesterday that they take Pippen to Showtime Pizza or bowling. He wanted more from her but that wasn't a surprise. He'd told her what he wanted from beginning. *All of you*, he'd said, but she wasn't real clear what that meant. All of her for now? Until she turned forty? "I have a ten-year-old son, and I'm trying to run my own business. I just want a peaceful, calm life and Tucker is complicated." But *was* Tucker complicated? Maybe, but more accurately, their relationship was complicated. A better word to describe Tucker was *relentless*.

"How?"

"He was in the Army and he saw a lot. He says he used to be closed off but isn't anymore." There were things he was keeping to himself. She hadn't a clue what those things were. Things that might have to do with his military experience or childhood or God knew what. "But for a man who says he isn't closed off anymore, he doesn't share a lot about himself." But neither did she.

For another hour, she wove color through Sadie's hair. They chatted about growing up in Lovett and Sadie's daddy, who'd been kicked by a horse and was currently a patient at the rehab hospital a few blocks from Lily's salon.

After she finished putting the color on Sadie's hair, she sat her under the salon dryer for twenty minutes and went to her office. She moved behind her desk and reached for the phone. "Thanks for the flowers," she said when Tucker's voicemail picked up. "They're gorgeous, but you really have to stop spending money on me."

She had an enormous pile of paperwork in front of her, invoices and business accounts to be paid. The sink in the aesthetician's room needed attention, and she called a plumber and scheduled an appointment. She finished Sadie Hollowell by trimming her straight hair and blowing it dry, giving it some texture and Texas sass.

After Sadie, her next appointment wanted a long, layered cut, preferred by most Texas women and Lily herself. The long, layered cut could be pulled back into a ponytail, loosely curled, or teased and stacked to Jesus. It was three o'clock when she finished, and she decided to grab all her paperwork and head home. It wasn't often that she could pick Pippen up after school, and she told her assistant manager she was leaving before she walked out the back door. It was almost sixty degrees and she shoved all her work into the backseat of her Jeep. As she pulled out of the parking lot, she called her mother.

"I'm off early enough to pick Pippen up from school," she said as she headed toward the highway.

"Okay. He'll like that." There was a pause and then her mother said, "He's been spending a lot of time playing basketball with that Deputy Matthews."

"Yeah, I know."

"Well, I don't know if it's such a good idea," Louella said.

"He's a nice man." With her eyes on the road, she fished around in her console for her sunglasses.

"We don't know that. We don't know him at all."

If her mother only knew how well Lily did know the

deputy. Knew he was good with his hands and liked to be ridden like Buster, the coin-operated horse outside Petterson's Drug. "He plays ball with Pippen in full view of everyone in the neighborhood, Ma. Pippen likes him, and let's face it, Pip spends way too much time with women. Spending time with a man is good for him."

"Huh." There was another pause on the line and Lily expected a rambling story about so and so's son who'd been molested by the Tastee Freeze man and had grown up to be a serial killer of biblical proportions. "Okay," she said.

"Okay?" No story? No rambling tale of disaster?

"Okay. If he's good to my grandson, then that's good enough for me."

Lily shoved her glasses on her face. Well, the world must have just officially ended. It wasn't exactly a ringing endorsement from her mother, but at least she wasn't accusing him of crimes against nature.

"Yesterday, my mom told me it's okay if you play with Pippen."

Tucker's brows pulled together and he handed Lily a plate he'd just rinsed. "You told her about us?"

Lily took the plate and set it in the dishwasher. "Not exactly, but she knows that sometimes you play ball with Pip when he gets home from school."

He reached for a kitchen towel and dried his hands. "What does 'not exactly' mean?"

Lily shut the door to the dishwasher. "It means I'll tell her. Just not now."

"Why?"

"Because she'll want to know everything about you," which was just *one* reason, but not the biggest one. "And you keep things to yourself. It makes me wonder what you're not telling me." There were things she had to figure out, like her feelings for him, and if she could trust the feelings he said he had for her. And if it all went south, could she handle it? "What deep dark secrets are you keeping from me? Did something happen in the military?"

He shook his head. "Being in the military saved my life."

"Tucker!" She pushed his shoulder but he didn't budge. "You were shot five times."

"I was shot *at* more than that." He smiled like it was no big deal. "That was just the last time. If not for the Army, I'd be dead or doing time in prison."

Prison? She took the towel from him and slowly dried her own hands. She looked closer at his smile, and a felt a somber blanketing of her heart. "Why do you say that?"

He turned away and reached into the refrigerator. "Before I enlisted, I was going nowhere and had nothing. I'd already done several years locked up in juvenile detention and was living in a youth home." He pulled out a half gallon of milk and moved toward the back door. "They kick you out at eighteen, but I was ready to leave anyway."

He knelt and poured milk into the empty cat dish. He wouldn't look at her so she moved to him and knelt beside him. "Where was your mother?"

"Dead," he said without emotion, but he wouldn't look at her. "Died of a drug overdose when I was a baby."

"Tucker." She put her hand on his shoulder, but he stood and moved to the refrigerator.

"Your daddy?" She rose and followed him.

"Never knew who he was. She probably didn't know either. I'm sure he was some crackhead like her."

"Who took care of you?"

"My grandmother, but she died when I was five." He put the milk inside and shut the door. "Then various aunts, but mostly the state of Michigan."

She thought of Pippen and her heart caved in her chest. "Tucker." She grabbed hold of his arm and made him look at her. "Every baby should be born into a living family. I'm sorry you weren't. That's horrible."

"It was fucked up, to be sure." He looked at the floor. "I lived in eleven different foster homes, but they were all the same: people just taking in kids to get money from the state. They were just a stopover to someplace else."

Honest to God, she didn't know what to say. She'd thought his secrets had something to do with . . . Well she hadn't known, but not this. Though it did explain some of his rough edges and why he might be relentless. "Why didn't you tell me?"

"People look at you differently when they find out no one wanted you as a kid. They look at you like something must be wrong with you. Like it's your fault."

She wanted to cry for this big, strong man who'd once been a lost boy, but felt she should be strong like him. The backs of her eyes stung and she blinked back her tears.

"I especially didn't want you to know."

"Why?"

"When people find out you've spent time in the juvenile jail, they look at you like you might steal the family heirlooms. No matter what else you do in your life."

She cupped his face in her hands and looked into his eyes. "I would never think that. I'm proud of you, Tucker. You should be proud of yourself. Look at you. You've overcome so much. It would have been easy and understandable if you'd gone bad, but you didn't."

"For a while I did. I stole everything I could get my hands on."

"Well, I don't have family heirlooms." She ran her hands across his shoulders, comforting him. "But maybe I should search you the next time you leave my house."

He flushed and cut his gaze to the side. "I would never steal from—"

"I'm going to like searching you too. Maybe I'll search you when you enter, just for good measure. Maybe I should search you right now."

He looked back at her, relief in his eyes. "But this is my house."

She shrugged. "I just don't think I should pass up a good opportunity to search you. Never know what I might find."

"I know what you'll find." He pulled her against his chest. "Start with the right front pocket."

She did and found him hard and ready for sex.

"Are you on birth control?" he asked, his voice going all smoky.

She thought it an odd question at this stage. "I've had an

IUD for about seven years now." Ever since a pregnancy scare when Pip had been three.

"Do you trust me?"

"With what?"

"I had to have a complete medical exam before I joined the Potter County Sherriff's office. Top to bottom. I'm clean. Do you trust me?"

He was asking to have sex without a condom. To take their relationship to the next step, and she wanted it so much it scared her. If they took things slow, maybe everything would work out. "Yes. Do you trust me?"

"Yes." He took her hand and led her to his bedroom. He kissed and touched and undressed her. He made love to her whole body, and when he entered her, hot and throbbing skin to skin, she moaned and arched her back. He cupped her face in his hands and looked into her eyes as he plunged in and out of her body. "Lily," he whispered. "I love you."

Complete euphoria rushed through her blood and heated her whole body. He said he loved her and she felt it in every part of her body. The euphoric feeling stayed with her long after she left his house that morning. Long after she went to work and returned home that night. She woke with it, but when she returned home after dropping Pippen off at school, her happy euphoric bubble got shot all to hell.

She pulled her Jeep into the garage just as Tucker was getting home from work. It was garbage day and she walked out to the curb to pull her empty can inside.

Tucker being Tucker, he met her in the driveway and

pulled it inside for her. She quickly shut the garage door and he followed her into the kitchen.

A smile played at the corner of her mouth. "Want coffee?"

"What are you doing tomorrow night? I have it off. I thought we could go to Ruby's. Some of the guys said Ruby's serves a good steak but to avoid the seafood."

Ruby's? Her smile fell. A restaurant in the middle of downtown Lovett—where the news that she was dating young Deputy Matthews would reach everyone by dessert. That wasn't taking things slow. What she felt was so new, she wasn't ready for that. "I have Pip."

"Can't he stay with your mom or sister for a few hours."

"That's awfully short notice, Tucker."

He folded his arms over his beige work shirt. "What about Sunday?"

"I don't know." He was pushing her. She understood him, but there was so much to think about. Everything was happening too fast. He said he loved her, but could she let herself love him as much as he deserved? That crazy kind of love that consumed and burned? She was too old and had too much to lose to love like that again. "I have a lot of work."

"Monday."

"How about someplace in Amarillo." That was a nice compromise. "The restaurants are better in Amarillo."

"No. How about Ruby's?"

"Why?"

"Because I'm tired of hiding. I want a whole life with you. You and Pip."

"You're young. How do you even know what you want?

When I was thirty, I thought I wanted something different than I want now."

"Quit treating me like a kid. I might be eight years younger than you, but I've lived a lot of different lives—enough of them to know what I want and what I don't want. I love you, Lily. I told you that and I meant it. I want to be with you. I'm into you one hundred percent, but if you aren't, you need to tell me. I'm no one's secret. Either you're in one hundred percent with me, or I'm out."

Out? A panicky little bubble lifted her stomach. "It's been just a little over a month!"

"It's been almost two months since I fell in love with you that first morning I saw you with curlers in your hair and bunny slippers on your feet. Knowing you love someone doesn't take time. It doesn't take ten years or ten months to figure it out. It takes looking across a driveway and feeling like you've been hit in the chest—like you can't breathe."

Out? Her head spun and the panicky bubble grew in her abdomen. Love made her impulsive and emotional and irrational. It made her panicky and crazy, and she'd worked so hard to be rational and sane. She didn't want to be crazy, but she didn't want to let him go. She was so conflicted she couldn't think, and she hated that feeling. It brought back all sorts of other feelings and memories . . . of pain and betrayal and hair-pulling fights. "I need a little more time."

He shook his head. "I'm not waiting around for the crumbs from your table. I spent my whole childhood doing that. The outsider looking in. Waiting. Wanting what would never be mine. I can't do it anymore, Lily." He folded his arms over his chest. "Are you in or out? It's that simple."

There was so much to think about. Her. Pip. What if he left her after a few months or years? Would she survive this time? Would she lose her mind again? "Why are you so stubborn about this?"

"I'm not stubborn, Lily. I just know what I want. If you don't want the same thing, if you don't want to be with me, you need to tell me now. Before I get in any deeper and start thinking I can have things that I can't."

"It's not that easy, Tucker. You can't expect me to make a decision right this very second."

"You just did."

CHAPTER EIGHT

"Are you still playing basketball with Deputy Matthews?" It had been three days since she'd seen Tucker. He hadn't even tried to contact her. She'd dialed him up twice, but he hadn't picked up or returned her call.

Pippen nodded as he snapped Legos together. "I almost beat him at H-O-R-S-E today."

She felt empty and envious—envious of her own son because he got to see Tucker. It was Saturday night. She should be relaxed and happy. Her salon was doing great, her son was fine, and she had the next two days off. Instead of relaxed, she felt edgy and ready to jumpy out of her own skin. "Do you like him?"

"Yeah, and Pinky too."

He wanted a life with her. He wanted her to jump in with both feet or not at all. "Did you go into his house?"

Pippen shook his head. "Pinky got out and ran into our backyard like Griffin used to. I took her back 'cause she's little and has no survival skills."

She thought of Tucker pouring milk into a little cat bowl.

Most of the men she knew said they hated cats. Only a supremely confident man would own one named Pinky. "What would you think if we had Tucker come over for dinner sometimes?" His confidence was one of the things she liked about him.

"Can we have pizza?"

"Sure."

"And maybe he could come with us when go bowling," her son suggested and snapped some sort of wings on the Legos. "He'll probably win, though."

Probably. Both she and Pip sucked. In the past, Pippen had always nagged her to call Ronnie to go bowling with them. "What about your dad?"

Pippen shrugged. "He has a new girlfriend. So, I probably won't see him for a while."

A sad smile twisted her lips as her heart hurt for her son. Ten years old and he had Ronnie Darlington all figured out. "What if I went out on a date with Tucker? If he took me out to dinner or something. Just him and me. Would that bother you?" she asked, even though she wasn't positive that Tucker would ever speak to her again. She remembered the look in his eyes the last time she'd seen him. Sad. Final.

He snapped a few more Legos together. "No. Are you going to kiss him?"

She'd like to kiss him. "Probably."

He made a face. "Grown-ups do gross stuff. I don't want to go to high school."

High school? "Why?"

"That's when people have to start kissin'. T.J. Briscoe told me his older brother rolls around kissin' his girlfriend until his parents come home from work."

There would come a day when Pip's thinking would radically change. Thank God she had a few more years before that happened. "Well, you don't have to kiss anyone if you don't want to." Lily bit the corner of her lip to keep from smiling. "Except me."

She rose from the couch and moved into the kitchen. She looked through the window at Tucker's house. The lights were out and he was no doubt working. Hiding in one of his favorite spots, waiting for unsuspecting speeders.

For the past few days he'd been avoiding her. He'd been honest about his life. He'd told her everything because he loved her. She hadn't been quite so honest. She hadn't told him everything because . . . she hadn't wanted him to leave her.

She closed her eyes and pressed her fingers into her brows. She hadn't been open and honest because she hadn't wanted him to leave, but he'd left anyway. She hadn't wanted to date him because of his age. She'd been afraid of what people would say. He hadn't cared. He'd been bold and fearless. She used to be bold and fearless. She used to love with her whole heart, like Tucker.

She lowered her hands and looked at his empty house. Her heart got all pinchy and achy. She did love him. She'd fought it, but she loved him with her whole pinchy, achy heart. Loved him so much it crawled across her skin and brought tears to her eyes. Her head got all light and anxious. She couldn't control her feelings. They were too big—too much—but unlike her thirty-year-old self she wasn't losing it. She couldn't control loving Tucker, but she wasn't out of control. She knew exactly what she was doing when she grabbed her coat and purse.

"Pippy, I need to go somewhere."

"Where?"

She wasn't quite sure, but she had a good idea. "Just out for some air."

She called her mother and made up a lie about having forgotten something at her salon. When Louella walked in the door, Lily shoved her arms in her coat and walked out.

She jumped in her Jeep and headed to Highway 152. She wasn't crazy, she was going after what she wanted. What she'd been afraid to want for a long time.

Tucker had mentioned he liked to hang out behind the Welcome to Lovett sign, waiting for speeders. She drove past—and sure enough, a Potter County cruiser sat several feet behind the sign. She flipped a U, floored the gas pedal, and hit eighty as she passed. She was still in perfect control. Not feeling crazy at all. She glanced into the rearview mirror and saw nothing but the inky black night.

"Okay," she said, still in control and not the least crazy. She flipped another U and this time got up to ninety-six. She glanced into the rearview and smiled as the red, white, and blue lights lit up the Texas night. She pulled over and waited. She crossed her arms and stared straight ahead, waiting. Her heart thumping and her chest aching. If she wasn't careful, she might hyperventilate. A Maglite tapped her window and she hit the switch.

"Lily."

"Neal?" She stuck her head out the window and looked down the highway. "What are you doing here?"

"My job. What are you doing out here driving like your tail's on fire?"

"I'm looking for someone." If Tucker wasn't on highway 152, where was he?

"I need your driver's license, registration, and proof of insurance."

Lily gasped. "You're not giving me a ticket are you?"

"Yes, ma'am. You were doing ninety-eight."

Ninety-six, but who was counting. "I don't have time Neal," she said as she dug around in her jockey box. "Can you just mail it to me?" She found her registration and handed it over with her license and insurance card.

"No. I'll be right back."

"But . . ." She didn't have time to sit around. She glanced in her rearview mirror and watched him move to his car. She called Tucker on her UConnect but hung up when his voicemail answered. Where could he be? She didn't want to kick in the back door of a jewelry store on the off chance he'd respond. She wasn't *that* crazy. Yet.

Within a few minutes Neal returned. "Sign here," he said and shined his light on a ticket clipped to a board.

"I still can't believe you're giving me a ticket."

"I can't believe you sped by me twice. What the hell is wrong with you, girl?"

"I thought you were someone else." She signed the ticket and handed him back the pen.

"Who?"

He was going to find out anyway. "Deputy Matthews."

Neal rocked back on his heels and laughed. "Tucker?"

Lily didn't have a clue what was so funny. "We're dating." She raised a hand and dropped it back on the steering wheel. "Sort of."

"Poor bastard. Are you going to drive your Jeep into his house?"

"That's not funny, and I can't believe you're bringing that up." Actually she could. Neal had been one of the first responders that horrible night of infamy. And this was Lovett. No one could just let anything go.

"Tucker's at the Road Kill with some of the guys. It's Marty's birthday and someone got him a stripper. If you go there, don't get all crazy."

She frowned. "I don't get crazy anymore."

"Then why are you out here speeding up and down the highway?"

It might not look like it, but she was in control. "I'm not crazy."

He tore off the ticket and handed it to her.

"I thought you were my friend, Neal."

"I am. That's why I wrote you a ticket for one-twenty instead of one-eighty-five like you deserve."

Lily gasped once more. "One hundred and twenty dollars?" She stuffed the ticket in her coat pocket.

"Good to see you, Lily."

"Wish I could say the same." What a jerk, but she had been raised right so she grudgingly added, "Tell Suzanne and the kids I said hey."

"Will do and slow down." Neal stepped back and Lily eased the Jeep back onto the highway. The Road Kill was about twenty minutes away and she was careful to drive the speed limit. She even drove a few miles under, but her mind raced—spinning and tumbling, and her heart felt like it was cracking. She was in love with Tucker. She took a deep breath and let it out, checking herself. She felt okay. Still not feeling crazy. Okay, maybe a tiny bit, but not enough to drive her car through someone's house *crazy*. That *was* crazy. Destructive crazy, and she wasn't that Lily anymore.

The gravel parking lot of the Road Kill was filled, but she was able to find a spot near the front door. She'd just go in, tell Tucker she loved him, and everything would work out. It had to . . . because she didn't want to think about a life without him in it.

Honky-tonk music filtered through the cracks in the building and grew louder when she went inside. Everyone knew that the back rooms could be rented out, and she headed through the bar. A few people called out her name and she held up a hand and waved as she wove her way through the crowd. When she got to one of the back rooms, she slipped through the door as a stripper in a cop outfit cuffed Marty Dingus to a chair. From an MP3 player, Kid Rock sang about picking up a "mean little missy" in Baton Rouge. Lily's gaze scanned the room until it landed on Tucker, who stood to one side. He wore a black T-shirt and jeans and his head was cocked to one side as if he was studying the stripper's butt.

Her heart pounding in her chest, Lily walked past the shocked gazes of some of the other deputies. Tucker was transfixed on the stripper and raised a bottle of Lone Star.

"Seriously, Tucker?" She stopped next to him. "Cadillac Pussy?" She pointed to the MP3 and the music blaring from the small speakers. "You know how I feel about crude language."

His head whipped toward her and he lowered the beer. "What are you doing here, Lily?" He looked shocked but not in the least ashamed.

"Apparently, I'm hunting you down." She turned her finger to the half-naked girl bumping and grinding. "And you're watching Marty get a lap dance."

Tucker shook his head. "She hasn't got to the lap dance part yet. That never happens until she strips to her G-string." He said it like it didn't even occur to him to be embarrassed that he knew that kind of information.

While she'd been out getting a ticket and acting a little impulsive, he'd been having a beer and watching a half-naked girl. Now . . . Now she was starting to feel a little crazy around the edges. "If you can drag yourself away from the sight of that stripper's butt, I'd like to have a few words with you. Outside?"

"Sure." He started through the small crowd of men and she slipped her hand into his. He looked back into her eyes and gave her hand a little squeeze that she felt in her heart. They moved down a short hall out the back door. A wooden deck had been built on the back of the bar, but this time of year it was empty.

Lily stopped next to a table turned on its side. She took a deep breath, past the big lump in her throat. Overhead light shined down on them, but his face gave nothing away.

She had to jump in now. All the way. "I love you, Tucker. I love you and I want to be with you." She swallowed hard and lowered her gaze to the dip in his throat. "You were honest with me and told me about your past and who you are, but I haven't told you about me." She shook her head and got the rest out in a rush of words. "Everyone thinks I'm crazy. I admit I've done a few crazy things in my past. Things that it took me a long time to live down, and I'm afraid once you know, you'll leave."

"I'm not going anywhere." He put a finger beneath her chin and raised her gaze to his. "I know who you are, Lily. I know all about you. I know you were one tick away from being 5150'd for driving your car into your ex's house. I know that you were knocked flat by him, but you pulled yourself up and made a success of yourself. You should be proud of yourself for that.

"I know that you love your son and the first time I saw you with Pippen, I saw *how much* you love him. You said you'd kill for him, and I knew that I wanted to love and be loved like that."

She blinked. "You know people call me crazy? Why didn't you say something?"

"Because it's not true. You're passionate and you love with your heart and soul, and I want that."

"What if it is true? I worked really hard not to be crazy, but I admit I'm feeling a little crazy right now. I got a speeding ticket tonight because I thought you were hiding behind the Welcome to Lovett sign."

"Whoa." He whipped he head back and forth. "What—"

"You've been ignoring me and I wanted to get your attention. So I raced up and down the highway." She pulled the ticket out of her pocket. "But it was Neal."

He tipped his head back and laughed. Long and loud, and then he gathered her against his chest. "You acted that crazy to get my attention?"

"Not *that* crazy. Just a *little* crazy."

"That's funny."

"Not really. Now Neal thinks I'm crazy again and he'll probably tell the guys you work with."

"I'm a big boy. I can handle anything as long as I have you."

"You do, Tucker, but it's not just me."

"I know, and I know I'm not Pippen's daddy. I can never be his daddy. Hell, I don't know how to be a dad, but I know that I'll never treat him mean or ignore him or leave him out. I'll never let him think he doesn't matter or disappoint him." If it was possible, her heart swelled more and she squeezed her arms around him. He pulled back and looked into her eyes. "I'd do anything for you, Lily, but I can't change my age."

"I know." She rose onto her toes and kissed the side of his neck. "I don't care."

He shivered. "You cared a lot a few days ago."

"A few days ago I was scared. I was afraid of what people would say. I was afraid of a lot of things, but you weren't. You were bold and unafraid."

"Are you kidding me? I've been scared shitless this whole time that you would never love me back."

He'd never acted scared—shitless or any other kind. "Two days ago you told me I had to get in or out." She lightly bit his ear. "I want in, Tucker. All of you. All the way." She dropped back on her heels and looked up into his face that was no longer free of expression. His smile was as big as hers.

"I want you all the way, Lily Darlington."

"People will say you're crazy."

"I don't care what people say." He pressed a quick kiss to her lips. "Just as long as I get to go crazy on you."

Read on for an excerpt from
New York Times bestselling author
Rachel Gibson's upcoming book

RESCUE ME

where you'll get to learn everything that happens
when Sadie Jo Hollowell returns to
Lovett, Texas!

On sale May 29, 2012
Only from Avon Books!

CHAPTER ONE

On December third, 1996, Mercedes Johanna Hollowell committed fashion suicide. For years, Sadie had teetered on the brink—mixing patterns and plaids while wearing white sandals after Labor Day. But the final nail in her fashion coffin, worse than the faux pas of white sandals, happened the night she showed up at the Texas Star Christmas Cotillion with hair as flat as roadkill.

Everyone knew the higher the hair, the closer to God. If God had intended women to have flat hair, He wouldn't have inspired man to invent styling mousse, teasing combs, and Aqua Net Extra Super Hold. Just as everyone knew that flat hair was a fashion abomination, they also knew it was practically a sin. Like drinking before Sunday service or hating football.

Sadie had always been a little . . . off. Different. Not batshit crazy different. Not like Mrs. London who collected cats and magazines and cut her grass with scissors. Sadie was more notional. Like the time she got the notion in her six-year-old head that if she dug deep enough, she'd strike gold.

As if her family needed the money. Or when she'd dyed her blond hair a shocking pink and wore black lipstick. That was about the time she'd quit volleyball, too. Everyone knew that if a family was blessed with a male child, he naturally played football. Girls played volleyball. It was a rule. Like an eleventh commandment: Female child shalt play volleyball or face Texas scorn.

Then there was the time she decided that the uniforms for the Lovett High dance team were somehow sexist and petitioned the school to lower the fringe on the Beaverettes' unitards. As if short fringe was a bigger scandal than flat hair.

But if Sadie was notional and contrary, no one could really blame her. She'd been a "late-in-life baby." Born to a hard-nosed rancher, Clive, and his sweetheart of a wife, Johanna Mae. Johanna Mae had been a Southern lady. Kind and giving, and when she'd set her cap for Clive, her family, as well as the town of Lovett, had been a little shocked. Clive was five years older than she and as stubborn as an old mule. He was from an old, respected family, but truth be told, he'd been born cantankerous and his manners were a bit rough. Not like Johanna Mae. Johanna Mae had been a beauty queen, winning everything from Little Miss Peanut to Miss Texas. She'd come in second place in the Miss America pageant the year she'd competed. She would have won if judge number three hadn't been a feminist sympathizer.

But Johanna Mae had been as shrewd as she'd been pretty. She believed it didn't matter if your man didn't know the difference between a soup bowl and a finger bowl. A good woman could always teach a man the difference. It just mattered that he could afford to buy both, and Clive Hollowell certainly had the money to keep her in Wedgwood and Waterford.

After her wedding, Johanna Mae had settled into the big house at the JH Ranch to await the arrival of children, but after fifteen years of trying everything from the rhythm method to in vitro fertilization, Johanna Mae was unable to conceive. The two resigned themselves to their childless marriage, and Johanna Mae threw herself into her volunteer work. Everyone agreed that she was practically a saint, and finally at the age of forty, she was rewarded with her "miracle" baby. The baby had been born a month early because, as her mother always put it, "Sadie couldn't wait to spring from the womb and boss people around."

Johanna Mae indulged her only child's every whim. She entered Sadie into her first beauty pageant at six months, and for the next five years, Sadie racked up a pile of crowns and sashes. But due to Sadie's propensity to spin a little too much, sing a little too loud, and fall off the stage at the end of a step ball change, she never quite fulfilled her mother's dream of an overall grand supreme title. At forty-five, Johanna Mae died of unexpected heart failure, and her beauty queen dreams for her baby died with her. Sadie's care was left to Clive, who was much more comfortable around Herefords and ranch hands than a little girl who had rhinestones on her boots rather than cow dung.

Clive had done the best he could to raise Sadie up a lady. He'd sent her to Ms. Naomi's Charm School to learn the things he didn't have the time or ability to teach her, but charm school could not take the place of a woman in the home. While other girls went home and practiced their etiquette lessons, Sadie shucked her dress and ran wild. As a result of her mashed education, Sadie knew how to waltz, set a table, and converse with governors. She could also swear like a cowboy and spit like a ranch hand.

Shortly after graduating from Lovett High, she'd packed up her Chevy and headed out for some fancy university in California, leaving her father and soiled cotillion gloves far behind. No one saw much of Sadie after that. Not even her poor daddy, and as far as anyone knew, she'd never married. Which was just plain sad and incomprehensible because really, how hard was it to get a man? Even Sarah Louise Baynard-Conseco, who had the misfortune to be born built like her daddy, Big Buddy Baynard, had managed to find a husband. Of course, Sarah Louise had met her man through prisoner.com. Mr. Conseco currently resided fourteen hundred miles away in San Quentin, but Sarah Louise was convinced he was totally innocent of the offenses for which he'd been unjustly incarcerated, and planned to start her family with him after his hoped-for parole in ten years.

Bless her heart.

Sure, sometimes in a small town it was slim pickings, but that's why a girl went away to college. Everyone knew that a single girl's number one reason for college wasn't higher education, although that was important, too. Knowing how to calculate the price of great-grandmother's silver on any given day was always crucial, but a single gal's first priority was to find herself a husband.

And Tally Lynn Cooper, Sadie Jo's twenty-year-old cousin on her mama's side, had done just that. Tally Lynn had met her intended at Texas A&M and was set to walk down the aisle in a few short days. Tally Lynn's mama had insisted that Sadie Jo be a bridesmaid, which in hindsight turned out to be a mistake. More than the choice of Tally Lynn's gown, or the size of her diamond, or whether Uncle Frasier would lay off the sauce and behave himself, the burning question on everyone's mind was if Sadie Jo had managed to snag herself a man yet because really, how hard could it be? Even for a contrary and notional girl with flat hair?

Sadie Hollowell hit the button on the door panel of her Saab and the window slid down an inch. Warm air whistled through the crack, and she pushed the button again and lowered the window a bit more. The breeze caught several strands of her straight blond hair and blew them about her face.

"Check that Scottsdale listing for me." She spoke into the BlackBerry pressed to her cheek. "The San Salvador three-bedroom." As her assistant, Renee, looked up the property, Sadie glanced out the window at the flat plains of the Texas panhandle. "Is it listed as pending yet?" Sometimes a broker waited a few days to list a pending sale with the hopes another agent would show a property and get a bit more. Sneaky bastards.

"It is."

She let out a breath. "Good." In the current market, every sale counted. Even the small commissions. "I'll call you tomorrow." She hung up and tossed the phone in the cup holder.

Outside the window, smears of brown, brown, and more brown slid past, broken only by rows of wind turbines in the distance, their propellers slowly turning in the warm Texas winds. Childhood memories and old emotions slid through her head one languid spin at a time. She felt the old mixed bag of emotions. Old emotions that always lay dormant until she crossed the Texas border. A confusion of love and longing, disappointment and missed opportunity.

Some of her earliest memories were of her mother dressing her up for a pageant. The memories had blurred with age, the over-the-top pageant dresses and the piles of fake hair clipped to her head were just faded recollections. She remembered the feelings, though. She remembered the fun and excitement and the comforting touch of her mother's hand. She remembered the anxiety and fear. Wanting to do well. Wanting to please, but never quite pulling it off. She remembered the disappointment her mother tried and failed to hide each time her daughter won best "pet photo" or "best dress" but failed to win the big crown. And with each pageant, Sadie tried harder. She sang a little louder, shook her hips a little faster, or put an extra kick into her routine, and the more she tried, the more she went off key, off step, or off the stage. Her pageant teacher always told her to stick to the routine they'd practice. Go with the script, but of course she never did. She'd always had a hard time doing and saying what she'd been told.

She had a wispy memory of her mother's funeral. The organ music bouncing off the wooden church walls, the hard white pews. The gathering after the funeral at the JH, and the lavender-scented bosoms of her aunts. "Poor orphaned child," they'd cooed between bites of cheese biscuits. "What's going to happen to my sister's poor orphaned baby?" She hadn't been a baby or an orphan.

The memories of her father were more vivid and defined. His harsh profile against the endless blue of the summer sky. His big hands throwing her into a saddle and her hanging on as she raced to keep up with him. The weight of his palm on top of her head, his rough skin catching in her hair as she stood in front of her mother's white casket. His footsteps walking past her bedroom door as she cried herself to sleep.

Her relationship with her father had always been confusing and difficult. A push and pull. An emotional tug of war that she always lost. The more emotion she showed, the more she tried to cling to him, and the more he pushed her away until she gave up.

For years she'd tried to live up to anyone's expectations of her. Her mother's. Her father's. Those of a town filled with people who had always expected her to be a nice, well-behaved girl with charm. A beauty queen. Someone to make them proud like her mother or someone to look up to like her father, but by middle school she'd tired of that heavy task. She'd laid down that burden, and just started being Sadie. Looking back, she could admit that she was sometimes outrageous. Sometimes on purpose. Like the pink hair and black lipstick. It wasn't a fashion statement. She hadn't been trying to find herself. It was a desperate bid for attention from the one person on the planet who looked at her across the dinner table night after night but never seemed to notice her.

The shocking hair hadn't worked, nor the string of bad boyfriends. Mostly, her father had just ignored her.

It had been fifteen years since she'd packed her car and left her hometown of Lovett far behind. She'd been back as often as she could. Christmases here and there. A few Thanksgivings, and once for her aunt Ginger's funeral. That had been five years ago.

Her finger pushed the button and the window slid all the way down. Guilt pressed the back of her neck and wind whipped her hair as she recalled the last time she'd seen her father. It had been about three years ago, when she'd lived in Denver. He'd driven up for the National Western Stock Show.

She pushed the button again and the window slid up. It didn't seem like that long since she'd seen him, but it had to have been because she'd moved to Phoenix shortly after that visit.

It might seem to some as if she was a rolling stone. She'd lived in seven different cities in the past fifteen years. Her father liked to say she never stayed in one place long because she tried to put down roots in hard soil. What he didn't know was that she never tried to put down roots at all. She liked not having roots. She liked the freedom of packing up and moving whenever she felt like it. Her latest career allowed her to do that. After years of higher education, moving from one university to another and never earning a degree in anything, she'd stumbled into real estate on a whim. Now she had her license in three states and loved every minute of selling homes. Well, not every moment. Dealing with lending institutions sometimes drove her nutty.

A sign on the side of the road ticked down the miles to Lovett and she pushed the window button. There was just something about being home that made her feel restless and antsy and anxious to leave before she even arrived. It wasn't her father. She'd come to terms with their relationship a few years ago. He was never going to be the daddy she needed, and she was never going to be the son he always wanted.

It wasn't even necessarily the town itself that made her antsy, but the last time she'd been home, she'd been in Lovett for less than ten minutes before she'd felt like a loser. She'd stopped at the Gas and Go for some fuel and a Diet Coke. From behind the counter, the owner, Mrs. Luraleen Jinks, had taken one look at her ringless finger and practically gasped in what might have been horror if not for Luraleen's fifty-year, pack-a-day wheeze.

"Aren't you married, dear?"

She'd smiled. "Not yet, Mrs. Jinks."

Luraleen had owned the Gas and Go for as long as Sadie could recall. Cheap booze and nicotine had tanned her wrinkly hide like an old leather coat. "You'll find someone. There's still time."

Meaning she'd better hurry up. "I'm twenty-eight." Twenty-eight was young. She'd still been getting her life together.

Luraleen had reached out and patted Sadie's ringless hand. "Well, bless your heart."

She had things more figured out these days. She felt calmer, until a few months ago when she'd taken a call from her aunt Bess, on her mother's side, informing her that she was to be in the wedding of her young cousin Tally Lynn. It was such short notice she had to wonder if someone else had dropped out and she was a last-minute substitute. She didn't even know Tally Lynn, but Tally Lynn was family, and as much as Sadie tried to pretend she had no roots, and as much as she hated the idea of being in her young cousin's wedding, she hadn't been able to say no. Not even when the hot-pink bridesmaid's dress had arrived at her house to be fitted. It was strapless and corseted, and the short taffeta pickup skirt was so gathered and bubbled that her hands disappeared into the fabric when she put them to her sides. It wouldn't be so bad if she was eighteen and going to her prom, but her high school years were a distant memory. She was thirty-three and looked a little ridiculous in her prom/bridesmaid's dress.

Always a bridesmaid. Never a bride. That's how everyone would see her. Everyone in her family and everyone in town. They'd pity her, and she hated that. Hated that she still gave a damn. Hated that she didn't currently have a boyfriend to take her. Hated it so much she'd actually given some thought to renting a date. The biggest, best-looking stud she could find. Just to shut everyone up. Just so she wouldn't have to hear the whispers and see the sideway glances, or have to explain her current manless life, but the logistics of renting a man in one state and transporting him to another hadn't been real feasible. The ethics didn't trouble Sadie. Men rented women all the time.

Ten miles outside Lovett, a weather vane and a part of an old fence broke up the brown-on-brown scenery. A barbed wire fence ran along the highway to the rough log-and-wrought-iron entry to the JH Ranch. Everything was as familiar as if she'd never left. Everything but the black truck on the side of the road. A man leaned one hip into the rear fender, his black clothing blending into the black paint, a ball cap shading his face beneath the bright Texas sunlight.

Sadie slowed and prepared to turn up the road to her father's ranch. She supposed she should stop and ask if he needed help. The raised hood on the truck was a big clue that he did, but she was a lone woman on a deserted highway and he looked really big.

He straightened and pushed away from the truck. A black T-shirt fit tight across his chest and around his big biceps. Someone else would come along.

Eventually.

She turned onto the dirt road and drove through the gate. Or he could walk to town. Lovett was ten miles down the highway. She glanced in her rearview mirror as he shoved his hands on his hips and looked after her taillights.

"Damn." She stepped on the brake. In the state only a couple of hours and already the Texas in her reared its hospitable head. It was after six. Most people would be home from work by now, and it could be minutes or hours before someone else drove by.

But . . . people had cell phones. Right? He'd probably already called someone. Through the mirror, he raised one hand from his hip and held it palm up. Maybe he was in a dead zone. She checked to make sure her doors were locked and put the car into reverse. The early evening sunlight poured through the back window as she reversed out onto the highway, then drove up alongside the road toward the big truck.

The warm light bathed the side of his face as the man moved toward her. He was the kind of guy who made Sadie a little uncomfortable. The kind who wore leather and drank beer and crushed empties on their foreheads. The kind who made her stand a little straighter. The kind she avoided like a hot fudge brownie because both were bad news for her thighs.

She stopped and hit the power button on her door handle.

The window slowly lowered halfway, and she looked up. Way up past the hard muscle beneath his tight black T-shirt, his wide shoulders and thick neck. It was an hour past his five o'clock shadow, and dark whiskers shaded the bottom half of his face and his square jaw. "Trouble?"

"Yeah." His voice came from someplace deep. Like it was dragged up from his soul.

"How long have you been stuck out here?"

"About an hour."

"Run out of gas?"

"No," he answered, sounding annoyed that he might be confused for the kind of guy who'd run out of gas. Like that somehow insulted his masculinity. "It's either the alternator or timing belt."

"Could be your fuel pump."

One corner of his mouth twitched up. "It's getting fuel. No power."

"Where you headed?"

"Lovett."

She'd figured that since there wasn't much else down the road. Not that Lovett was much. "I'll call you a tow truck."

He raised his gaze and looked down the highway. "I'd appreciate it."

She punched the number to information and got connected with B.J. Henderson's garage. She'd gone to school with B.J.'s son, B.J. Junior, who everyone called Boner. Yeah, Boner. The last she'd heard, Boner worked for his dad. The answering machine picked up and she glanced at the clock in her dash. It was five minutes after six. She hung up and didn't bother to call another garage. It was an hour and five minutes past Lone Star time, and Boner and the other mechanics in town were either at home or holding down a barstool.

She looked up at the man, past that amazing chest, and figured she had two choices. She could take the stranger to her daddy's ranch and have one of her father's men take him into town, or take him herself. Driving to the ranch would take ten minutes up the dirt road. It would take twenty to twenty-five to take him into town.

She stared into the shadow cast over his profile. She'd rather a stranger didn't know where she lived. "I have a stun gun." It was a lie, but she'd always wanted one.

He looked back down at her. "Excuse me?"

"I have a stun gun and I've been trained to use it." He took a step back from the car and she smiled. "I'm deadly."

"A stun gun isn't a deadly weapon."

"What if I set it really high?"

"Can't set it high enough to kill unless there is a preexisting condition. I don't have a preexisting condition."

"How do you know all that?"

"I used to be in security."

Oh. "Well, it will hurt like hell if I have to zap your ass."

"I don't want my ass zapped, lady. I just need a tow into town."

"Garages are all closed." She tossed her phone in the cup holder. "I'll drive you into Lovett, but you have to show me some identification first."

Annoyance pulled one corner of his mouth as he reached into the back pocket of his Levi's, and for the first time, her gaze dropped to his five-button fly.

Good Lord.

Without a word, he pulled out a driver's license and passed it through the window.

Sadie might have cause to feel a little pervy about staring at his impressive package if it hadn't been sort of framed in her window. "Great." She punched up a few numbers on her cell and waited for Renee to pick up. "Hi, Renee. It's Sadie again. Gotta pen?" She looked at the hunk of man junk in front of her and waited. "I'm giving a stranded guy a ride into town. So, write this down." She gave her friend the Washington driver's license number and added, "Vincent James Haven. 4389 North Central Avenue, Kent, Washington. Hair: brown. Eyes: green. Six foot and a hundred and ninety pounds. Got it? Great. If you don't hear from me in an hour, call the Potter County sheriff's office in Texas and tell them I've been abducted and you fear for my life. Give them the information that I just gave you." She shut the phone and handed the ID through the window. "Get in. I'll drop you off in Lovett." She looked up into the shadow of his hat. "And don't make me use my stun gun on you."

"No ma'am." One corner of his mouth slid up as he took his driver's license and slid it back into his wallet. "I'll just get a duffel."

Her gaze dropped to the back pockets of his jeans as he turned and shoved his wallet inside. Nice chest. Great butt, handsome face. If there was one thing she knew about men, one thing she'd learned from being single all these years, it was that there were several different types of men. Gentlemen, regular guys, charming dogs, and dirty dogs. The only true gentlemen in the world were purebred nerds who were gentlemen in the hopes of someday getting laid. The man grabbing a duffel from the cab of his truck was too good-looking to be a purebred anything. He was likely one of those tricky hybrids.

She hit the door locks, then he tossed a green military duffel into the backseat. He got in the front, and set off the seat belt alarm, filling up the Saab with his broad shoulders and the annoying *bong bong bong* of the belt alarm.

She put the car into drive, then pulled a U-turn out onto the highway. "Ever been to Lovett, Vincent?"

"No."

"You're in for a treat." She pulled on a pair of sunglasses and stepped on the gas. "Put on your seat belt, please."

"Are you going to zap me with your stun gun if I don't?"

"Possibly. Depends on how annoyed I get by the seat belt alarm between here and town." She adjusted the gold aviators on the bridge of her nose. "And I should warn you in advance, I've been driving all day, so I'm already annoyed."

He chuckled and belted himself in. "You headed to Lovett yourself?"

"Unfortunately." She glanced at him out of the corners of her eyes. "I was born and raised here but I escaped when I was eighteen."

He pushed up the bill of his hat and looked across his shoulder at her. His driver's license had stated that his eyes were green and they were. A light green that wasn't quite spooky. More unsettling, as he stared back at her from that very masculine face. "What brings you back?" he asked.

"Wedding." Unsettling in a way that made a girl want to twist her hair and put on some red lip gloss. "My cousin's getting married." Her younger cousin. "I'm a bridesmaid." No doubt the other bridesmaids were younger, too. They'd probably arrive with a date. She'd be the only single one. Old and single. A "Welcome to Lovett, Texas, Y'all" sign marked the city limits. It had been painted a bright blue since the last time she'd been home.

"You don't look happy about it."

She'd been out of Texas too long if her "uglies" were showing. According to her mother, "uglies" were any emotions that weren't pretty. A girl could have them. Just not show them. "The dress is meant for someone ten years younger than me and is the color of Bubble Yum." She glanced out the driver's side window. "What brings you to Lovett?"

"Pardon?"

She glanced at him as they passed a used car lot and a Mucho Taco. "What brings you to Lovett?"

"Family."

"Who're your people?"

"Person." He pointed to the Gas and Go across the street. "You can drop me off there."

She cut across two lanes and pulled into the parking lot. "Girlfriend? Wife?"

"Neither." He squinted and looked out the windshield at the convenience store. "Why don't you go ahead and call your friend Renee, and tell her you're still in one piece."

She pulled to a stop in an empty slot next to a white pickup and reached into the cup holder. "Don't want the sheriff knocking on your door?"

"Not on my first night." He unbuckled the belt and opened the passenger door. His feet hit the pavement and he stood.

She could practically smell the popcorn from the Gas and

Go as she punched in Renee's number. Lady Gaga's "Born This Way" played in her ear until her assistant answered. "I'm not dead." Sadie pushed her sunglasses to the top of her head. "I'll see you in the office on Monday."

The rear door opened and he pulled out his duffel. He dumped it on the curb, then closed the door. He placed his hands on the roof of the car, then leaned down and looked through the car at her. "Thanks for the ride. I appreciate it. If there's any way I can repay you, let me know."

It was the kind of thing people said and never meant. Like asking, "How are you?" when no one really gave a crap. She looked across at him, into his light green eyes and dark masculine face. Everyone in town had always said she had more nerve than sense. "Well, there is one thing."

And if you want to read about Lily's sister, Daisy, don't miss DAISY'S BACK IN TOWN Available from Avon Books

About the Author

RACHEL GIBSON lives in Idaho with her husband, three kids, two cats, and a dog of mysterious origin. She began her fiction career at age 16, when she ran her car into the side of a hill, retrieved the bumper, and drove to a parking lot, where she strategically scattered the car's broken glass all about. She told her parents she'd been the victim of a hit-and-run and they believed her. She's been making up stories ever since, although she gets paid better for them nowadays.

Be Impulsive!

Look for Other
Avon Impulse Authors

www.AvonImpulse.com